The Awakening

The Boston Beginning

King Atlas V

Atlantean V Bookworks
Naples, FL

King Atlas V/Atlantean V Bookworks
P.O. Box 9651
Naples, FL 34101
https://www.amazon.com/author/kingatlasv

Publisher's Note: This is a work of fiction. Names, characters, places, and incidents are a product of the author's imagination. Locales and public names are sometimes used for atmospheric purposes. Any resemblance to actual people, living or dead, or to businesses, companies, events, institutions, or locales is completely coincidental.

Book Layout & Design ©2017 - BookDesignTemplates.com

Image   E-Book   Cover: Copyright: <a href="https://www.123rf.com/profile_edan">edan / 123RF Stock Photo</a>

The Awakening/ King Atlas V -- 1st ed.
ISBN Ebook 978-0-9985856-6-6; ISBN Paperback 978-0-9985856-7-3

Dedicated to St. Aloysius

Healing is a miracle

–Unknown

Table of Contents

1.

THE CHARLES RIVER was frozen solid. A blanket of white snow covered it from bank to bank. It was just past dusk, on the day after Christmas, a Thursday. The sky was dark, the dim starlight of deep winter not yet strong enough to sparkle through the cityscape glow. Traffic was light but steady on Storrow and Memorial Drives, the automobile head beams a moving string of holiday lights strung along each side of the river. A lonely runner dashed on the snow-packed path along Storrow Drive, keeping her balance, and knifing through the bitterly cold wind. The snow pack was even in height with the fence that guarded Storrow Drive after another bombogenesis storm had dumped two feet of snow onto Boston. The girl glided on the path like a winter reindeer.

Nearby, a small girl held her ragged, worn but loving little teddy bear tightly to her chest. She watched the jogger from her bed through the tiny back bedroom window of her Grandmother's fifth floor apartment on Beacon Street, near the intersection with Gloucester Street. She watched the peaceful, rhythmic and determined stride of the lonely fe-

male jogger. It lulled her into a softer state of consciousness. The jogger's steady glide masked her peril of running
so close to the road on the deep snow pack with no protec-
tion from the snow-covered fence.

The little girl's pain was gone now, the steady flow into
her system of the special IV fluids made sure of that. In a
few moments, she would head back to St. Aloysius Hospital
in Boston. She hoped it was to live longer, but knew it was
to spend her final hours. Her plan had been to die in her
Grandmother's home under hospice care. But her Grandmother had fallen gravely ill and was taken to another hospital the night before. Her Grandmother had called St.
Aloysius to readmit her. She was with her hospice nurse,
waiting for her departure.

She looked to the sky, and thought she saw one tiny
twinkle. *Surely, my guardian angel has arrived! To heal me? Or to
whisk me away! Hopefully, I will make it back to the hospital to say
goodbye to my friends. I was supposed to die with my Grandmother, but being with my friends, I like that. They know I am just going
to the other side.*

The little girl saw flashing red lights reflect off her window panes. She knew the ambulance had arrived on Back
Street, below her window. The nurse held her hand tightly
and removed her IV. Two paramedics soon were in the
room, with a gurney, to take her away. She was ready. She
glanced out her window one last time at the Charles River.
Oddly, cars were stopped on Storrow Drive. People were
getting out of their cars. She saw a heap, in front of one of
the cars. Others were on their cell phones, appearing fran-
tic. The hospice nurse looked out as well. The paramedics
were suddenly gone.

The little girl started to cry. The nurse covered her
mouth in shock. The nurse had opened the window slightly
ajar. Two women were frantically screaming that a young

woman jogger had slipped and fallen onto the road in front of a passing car. They were shrieking for help.

The little girl shouted as loud as she could through the tiny crack of her mouth and tiny slit of the open window.

"HELP HER!"

The two paramedics crossed the road to the fallen jogger. Because of the deep snow they were able to climb over a fence on to Storrow Drive.

Bystanders urged them to hurry.

The little girl stopped crying. She saw a white light flash from the sky, and then a white glow. The bystanders were briefly focused on the two paramedics, and missed the light and glow.

But the little girl focused on the white glow. A soft white glow. A man in a winter overcoat and Patriots pullover winter cap was leaning over the young female jogger. She saw him hold his right hand over her heart. She saw more white light emanate from his hand and into the jogger's chest. A slight movement of the jogger's head tipped her off that the something special had happened. The jogger grabbed both sides of the man's face with her open palms. The little girl thought she saw actual joy in physical form bond the two. Soon the man was gone. Hidden in the shadows.

The jogger stood. The bystanders were stunned and disbelieving what they saw. A mangled body, now in pure form, stood defiantly before them. Their memories and the sight of her torn and blood-stained clothing tugged at the reality before them. The crowd dispersed. The paramedics brought her back with them to the ambulance. She was soon released. She went to a nearby coffee shop.

The paramedics then fetched the young girl. She was beaming. She knew.

2.

THE SMALL GIRL LAY IN HER BED IN ROOM 1010 ON THE TENTH AND TOP FLOOR OF ST. ALOYSIUS HOSPITAL FOR LOST AND FORGOTTEN CHILDREN. A nurse had tucked her in and walked back to the nurses' central station. She heard the nurse and a second nurse chatting with the two paramedics, who had stayed for a cup of coffee, shaken about the strange turn of events on Storrow Drive. But the paramedics never mentioned the man, nor any white glow or white light. *Surely, they had seen the man and the white light. But, maybe not.*

The paramedics were amazed the female jogger had survived her fall into traffic with torn clothes as the only apparent casualty. But they were silent. They could not explain the blood on the pavement, the snowbank and her clothes. A passing animal? Maybe the jogger was bleeding, and they missed it?

The small girl, still able to ambulate, slid from her bed, left her room and walked a few feet to look out a window at the end of the hall. She gazed up at the sky. She could now see a silvery moon, and tiny twinkling stars. She had watched a holiday classic movie that morning.

Maybe an angel earned his wings today!

Her mind raced. *Why would the jogger run so closely to the roadway in such slippery and wintery conditions? Maybe she had jumped into the road, and the angel had saver her, like in the movie? Or maybe she really just slipped or lost track of where she was? So healthy, so young, so athletic, surely, it was an accident. If only I were so healthy.*

The little girl walked back to her room. It was one of ten rooms on the tenth floor. All the kids were asleep, all on life's final ticks, and all on various forms of painkillers to ease their final days.

St. Aloysius Hospital overlooked the Charles River and sat on a small plot of land donated to the hospital. It was west of Kenmore Square, just off of Commonwealth Avenue. A bridge over the Charles River was just across the way, as was a footbridge. A boathouse was visible from the top floors on the other side of the Charles River off of Memorial Drive. A small extension road off of Commonwealth Avenue had been constructed for access to the hospital. The hospital devoted most of its resources to severely ill children. It had a remarkable success rate at helping children, but still many succumbed, including almost all of those on the tenth floor.

The little girl's mind was very active and she was still ambulatory, but her organs were within moments of shutting down from an undiagnosed and evidently very rare condition. She never knew when her last breath might be taken. She had already lived longer than she was supposed to, by three days. That is what the hospice nurse told her.

How many more days or hours?

She turned on her television. NO stories about a jogger struck on the road. *Was it an illusion? But the nurse talked about it, and so did the paramedics. She was hit. But what of the man? Is he an angel?*

Then a new story. A funny thing had just happened that evening. Two men, one dressed like an elf, and one like Santa, apparently were stranded on the frozen Charles River on the east side of the bridge near the hospital. Some thought they had too much holiday cheer. They appeared to walk aimlessly, trying to find the best way back to shore. The ice was thick and deeply snow covered, so they were safe. A dog, a golden retriever, had gone out to fetch them. Cameras had followed their follies, until they went to shore near the boathouse, the one that she could see from her window. They had disappeared after that. No interviews, no questioning. The little girl recognized the boathouse. Her late mother had crewed in college, and she knew all the boathouses on the Charles River. Television viewers secretly pined that it was really an elf and really Santa.

She shut off the television. She walked back to the window. She stared at the boathouse. No elf and no Santa. Where were they, she wondered. She gazed for a while. She saw two wheelchairs, abandoned near the back of the boathouse. Her mind had no current thoughts on the matter, but the sight of the wheelchairs was filed away for later review.

Tomorrow, if she were still alive, she would try to see some of her friends. They had all said their final good-byes to her when she left for her Grandmother's. Oddly, no one had gone to the other side since she had left. This time of year, it was sad. None of the kids in the hospital had family. Kids with family did not go to St. Aloysius. Once the holidays had passed, no one visited them. They had some well-wishers and good doers visit them during the holiday period, including local college and professional athletes. But once Christmas passed by, they stopped. Not so oddly, the kids seemed to flourish and survive during those two weeks. But then sadness set in, and most of the kids died within weeks. This is what she had heard and knew deep down.

But, tomorrow there will be hope.

3.

MARCUS JACKSON, AFFECTIONATELY KNOWN AS JACKHAMMER, was Boston's new sensation on talk radio. His ratings were off the charts. His show was number one in its time slot by a considerable margin. He had moved to Boston from the Midwest fifteen months ago. Raised and educated in Nebraska, he was a star on Omaha talk radio. He moved to Boston to live near his only sister and to be with his former fiancé who was attending an elite business school. She had dumped him within a month of his arrival for one of her adoring classmates, with Ivy League credentials. Now, at 29 years of age, he focused all his energy on his show. His show was dynamic and entertaining, as well as informative. His personality seemed larger than life. He covered politics, sports, entertainment and current events. He was bombastic at times, and compassionate at times. He had his detractors and bashers, but far more adoring fans. His market included radio listeners, commuters, and a phalanx of office and at-home workers and others, who had his station on in the background with live streaming on their smart speakers.

Jackhammer swashed down his coffee shop black coffee, chasing his breakfast down his gullet. He wiped his mouth and smiled at his young producer, Sandy, a young woman, with sandy blonde hair, from a local college, and former member of their women's lacrosse team. He was otherwise alone today, his show cohorts off for the holiday week in warmer climates or skiing up north or out west.

Sandy nodded, suggesting a lone caller was on hold. Sports were quiet today. The Patriots had a meaningless final game on the upcoming Sunday, where most of the starters would not play. A first round bye was secured. The Celtics and Bruins were off until Monday, and the hot stove for baseball was not very hot. No golf or tennis to talk about. Oddly, politics was quiet for once. There were no breaking scandals to harp on, and the entertainment industry was quiet, too. No compelling current events to speak of, either.

"It's a frigid day here in Boston, and the world seems so quiet! One lonely caller! Where are all my bashers, my detractors, my pundits and cynics? Are you all riding your reindeer back to the north pole? Yes, the north pole is real! Santa is real! He was on the Charles River last night! And his real-life elf! Ha! The two escaped before the authorities could capture them for questioning. Yes, the real Santa! But Santa is now gone! I saw his sled leave last night. Yeah, I saw a white light flash across the sky!"

Jackhammer smiled at Sandy. But he looked nervous, she thought.

"You know, I really did see a bright white light last night. I am sure it was nothing. But maybe it was something. But it was before the story of Santa and the elf broke. So, it wasn't Santa leaving on his sleigh! I don't know. There is something else, too," he said, looking at Sandy with an awkward smile.

"Pick up the caller, it's John from the South End," she responded, vexed by the revelation.

"First time caller, never a listener, Jackhammer, but I got a scoop for you, because everyone listens to you."

"Yeah, you know you are a long-time listener. I bet you listen every day!"

"Yeah, I do. But Jackhammer, I saw that bright white light last night, too!"

"See, folks, another witness to Santa leaving the Charles!" Jackhammer anxiously scoffed.

"But Jackhammer, listen, I am on Massachusetts Avenue. Crazy stuff is going on. There are all of these homeless folks singing and holding hands. They are surrounding five men and six women. They are singing holiday songs. I swear I saw another man in that circle, who then left. I saw a white light. I think the eleven were disabled or ill. They all seem healthy and happy now. Two of the women are shrieking. Hosanna! Hosanna!"

"What the bleep are you hallucinating about? Santa left last night. The angel got his wings last night. Ha! They are gone. They are not on Massachusetts Avenue. So, what do you really want to talk about, John the Baptist, from the South End!"

"Ha! Clever name. Honestly, dozens are now gathering. And praying and singing and wailing. It is scary, yet enlightening, and maybe, awakening. I think, I don't know. I have to go."

"So, fantasy, fiction, fancy, fable, folklore, mythology, fake news, daydreams, wishes, fairy tales, miracles, ghosts, spirits, angels, demons, aliens, messengers, prophets, divinity, it is all on the table, on this quiet cold Friday. Wait, the wind chill is minus ten. Snow banks are everywhere. Nobody should be on the streets!"

Jackhammer wiped the perspiration from his brow. Sandy brought him some more coffee.

"You look ghostly white! I have never seen you so shaken. What is going on?" Sandy watched him in earnest for an answer. Jackhammer searched her eyes, and then spilled his thoughts.

"There is something else. My sister said she was run over by a car last night on Storrow Drive. But an angel, maybe a man, touched her heart with his hand and healed her. There was a white glow, she thought. Her clothes are still bloodstained. She is freaked out. She mostly left her body, only a thread holding her on. The man disappeared. She only told me this, and she is now hiding in my condo in the Seaport. And what, Santa and an Elf? Were they real? No way, but what if? And now this Massachusetts Avenue cataclysmic event! Yeah, I am freakin' shaking, and I am pale white!"

Sandy freaked out herself.

"What are you talking about. Some sort of angel or alien or messenger from God! Is the Apocalypse coming!

4.

THE LITTLE GIRL HAD HER EARPHONES ON. She awoke late that morning. She strolled to her favorite window, the gateway to the world. She saw the wheelchairs by the boathouse, still there, empty. She saw the Charles River. She saw the letters carved in the snow near the bridge. She wondered if anyone else could see the letters. You could not see them from street level.

It was a little after 10 a.m. She was still alive. She had her favorite talking head on. She loved Jackhammer. She thought he was funny, even though he was sometimes rude. He was perceptibly smart and articulate to a fault. He was a wise-guy and a genius, who could debate with college profs, and smack talk with the tough guys. But she just loved his dynamic, bold, yet often compassionate character, and his booming laugh. It was a few hours to forget where she was.

But today she smiled. Jackhammer unknowingly had confirmed her beliefs. *What I saw was true. It is the same man on Massachusetts Avenue. It must be. Will he come see me? Yes, of course, I saw the white light from his hands. I saw the white flash of light before the accident. Not Santa! Ha! But that would be fun to believe! Why not? And a big elf. But I know they were not Santa and an Elf. Aha! Now I know. The wheel chairs. But where did they get the costumes?*

Her name was Anna. She called the number. She knew it by heart. She was Asian-American. Her late father, and his mother, her Grandmother on Beacon Street, were Yankees. Her late Mom, a local college grad, where she met her father, was from China. She missed her parents so much. All of her known relatives were on the other side, except her Grandmother. And the family fortune was long gone, wiped out when her father's family business went bust from technological obsolescence.

Sandy took the call.

"Hi, who is this? And what would you like to talk about?"

A faint voice drifted over the line.

"I am Anna. I saw an angel last night heal a woman jogger..."

Sandy dropped the line. She hyperventilated. Jackhammer ran to her. Commercials were running. He had a moment.

"Talk to Anna," Sandy barely whispered. Jackhammer rested his hand on her shoulder. It seemed to calm her.

"Hi Anna, this is Jackhammer. You are not on the air. What is up?" Jackhammer was aghast over what he might hear.

"Hi, first time caller, listener forever! I love you!"

Jackhammer relaxed. Another worshiper, idolizer, young girl with a crush. So many women adored him, he thought, his self-aggrandizement rearing its head, and taking him away for a moment.

"Thanks, Anna, but you sound awfully young, my dear!"

"Well, I am!"

"Anna, I have to go, what?"

"Last night, I saw a man place his hand over the heart of a young woman jogger after she fell onto Storrow Drive and was hit by a car. She looked dead to me. I saw a glow, a white light flow from his hand. She got up and walked away with my paramedics! The man healed her! Was it a miracle? Was he an angel? Santa? Who is he? Is he the man on Massachusetts Avenue?" Anna ran out of breath, and energy. It overwhelmed her to say what she had said, but also that Jackhammer had talked to her.

Jackhammer fell down to the floor on his knees. *A witness. His sister was telling the truth. But had she! Did she have this Anna call just to spook him? Was this a spoof for his show? Was Sandy behind this, to spark ratings on a boring holiday weekday show, too. Were Sandy and his sister and Anna in a big conspiracy with John the Baptist? Yes, of course. But what was the bright white light. And sis, she was frightened beyond belief. And she was never much of an actress, or liar, or a poker face.*

Jackhammer gathered himself. He saw new calmness in Sandy's eyes. Maybe she would fess up.

Sandy stayed quiet. She suspected Anna had seen someone special. Maybe an alien or an angel. Everything was on the table. The phone lines were now lit up. Jackhammer lit up. He loved to see the lines lit up. He nodded to Sandy to line up the calls.

5.

WINSTON ARRIVED at the coffee shop on Massachusetts Avenue. It was late morning, about 11 a.m., he reckoned, not caring to look for sure on his smartphone. A large man followed him into the shop. Winston watched him. Winston left his cap on. He took a big breath.

Memories of his healings in London swirled through his mind. The Crown, the London reporter and those that had been healed had kept the healings confidential and out of the public eye. He had returned to a normal life, his Connecticut friends keeping the secret as well. But he had been overwhelmed Christmas night with visions. Visions of an ancient continent. Visions of healing. Bright white lights. Lots of young children in need of healing. He awoke the day after Christmas, left his Connecticut home, and headed to the great city of Boston. He was going to go to St. Aloysius Hospital. He had parked in the Boston Common garage. He was walking along the Charles River on a snow packed path towards the hospital, when he heard a horrific shrieking and a horrible thud. He ran to the sound ahead. He saw that a young female jogger who had passed him seconds before had been struck by a car on Storrow Drive. Lying in a heap, he ran to her. Without thought or hesitation, he approached her. There was a flash of white light. Before her last breath could be exhaled, he placed his hand on her heart. There was more white light-a glow. She was healed. He felt shaken by the event and decided to grab a room for the night near Kenmore Square. Friday morning, he awoke. As if guided by an unknown force, he had walked down to Massachusetts Avenue, instead of to the hospital, and walked all the way to the entrance to the access road to Interstate 93.

Winston saw another man walk into the coffee shop. He was blind, using his walking stick. He had been in the doorway for a few moments. The large man watched Winston intently. Winston stared back at him, causing the large man to look away. Winston eyed the smartphone held by the large man. The large man appeared ready to snap a picture or a video. Winston walked over to him.

He placed his hand on the large man's shoulder. A white light hovered over his hand. The smartphone slipped from the large man's hand, bouncing on the wood floor. The large man shuddered. His life-long chronic back pain and joint pain from rheumatoid arthritis was gone. He trembled.

Winston walked over to the blind man who spoke to him.

"I have been waiting patiently for you, you know. Heard your thoughts on London. Just sayin'. Don't know who you are. Don't care. But I heard about stuff up on Massachusetts Avenue. People are better. People are healthy. Drug addiction is gone. Alcohol addiction is gone. Undernourishment is gone. Hope it stays that way. You are a King, I hear. Maybe a prophet, a messenger, an alien, or Santa, wait no suit. Or even a ghost. The holy ghost. Like I say, I don't care. I've been waiting for you. A long time. Since I was a boy, when I lost my sight."

Winston watched as the blind man shook as he spoke. He was clean shaven. He was showered. His clothes were old and soiled, though. His shoes had holes, his toes were exposed, and cold. His dark skin was glistening, a slight perspiration sneaking though his pores, even on a cold day.

Winston whispered into the blind man's ear. He put his right hand over his eyes. The large man, an African-American, watched in awe.

A white light glowed over his eyes. The man trembled. He kept his eyes closed. He hugged Winston tightly for a long moment. The large man watched intently-waiting for the anticipated outcome.

The blind man then opened his eyes. He saw a table, with some chairs. He saw a napkin holder, with brown nap-kins. He slowly turned his head. He saw a counter. He saw a waitress who was weeping, uncontrollably. He saw three cups of coffee, in cups, with tops on them. Steam was gen-tly streaming out of the small openings.

On cue, he let go of Winston. He took one cup of coffee and held it with both hands. He stared at it. He put his nose just above the cup. He let the aroma fill his nostrils. He took a big breath. He took a sip and sighed. He shook his head back and forth. And then he gazed outside the window.

Finally, he stepped out into the bright light of day. He turned, and smiled, like he hadn't in years. He raised his hands to the sky and screamed as loud as he had ever screamed. "Alleluia! Praise to the Lord! Hail to the King! Ho! Ho! Ho!"

The large man in the shop then hugged Winston, too. Winston grabbed the second cup of coffee, paid for three cups, and left the shop. He saw the large man take the third cup of coffee, and then attempt to take his picture, but he was not fast enough. Winston disappeared into the street, suddenly walking with dozens of passersby and revelers, who were celebrating the earlier healings. The man who used to be blind walked just ahead of him. Happiness and joy were spilling into the streets. Singing, praying and chanting, the revelers were in an ecstatic state, a joyous state, one that they had not felt, ever.

The large man, John from the South End, picked up his phone and then called Jackhammer. He waited patiently, overcome by a glow that filled his body.

"John, yes, I am one big ear. Crazy stuff indeed. I believe you, dude, I do. What more do you have?" Jackhammer asked confidently over the air for his listeners, but inside he was a mess. He trembled as he listened. Sandy watched in silence, mesmerized, and certain that there was a special force or being or something out there, this holiday week.

"Yes, I was going to tell you something. But, no, I will not. But maybe. I am well now. I am good. I am all right. I am ok. People are joyous down here. Never seen so many happy faces. It is getting crowded. Some people are saying long live the King. Other people are praying to the Lord. Other people are shouting out for their God. Other people are running and hiding from aliens. People are looking for help. They want to be helped, too. A mom carrying her sick child, just passed by, and is looking for... It is getting crazy! So many emotions! So much confusion of passersby and drivers. The drivers are asking what is going on. I saw it with my own eyes. I felt it in my own body and soul. I saw the white light. So there, I told you something. And I am not John the Baptist. I did not foretell of this, only about this. Bye. Bye! I am shaking too much to continue this talk."

"Wait! John?"

Jackhammer sat silently, not sure what to say next.

John from the South End meanwhile ran to the mom carrying her child.

"Come with me. I know where he is, who he is. Follow me. Quickly. Run with me."

The mom stopped shrieking. Her voice could not be heard above the din in any event. Her child was limp, quiet, seemingly lifeless in her arms.

"Is the child alive?"

"Yes, but not for long. He is dying. Is there really hope! Is there? Who are you? Are you John the Baptist that I heard on the radio with Jackhammer? If you had not called, I would not be here. You may have saved my son's life!" She fell back, out of breath.

"Stay here. Don't run."

John dashed ahead. He had seen Winston head to the left of the coffee shop, back towards the original healings. He caught Winston.

"Come with me. Just one small matter. Come."

Winston looked into the large man's eyes through to his soul. He agreed and followed him. No one knew who he was. He was just another older man walking the streets on a cold winter day. All were oblivious to him. They did not know what or who to look for. The revelers did not provide answers, they just kept singing and praying and chanting.

Finally, they arrived. Winston saw the child, hanging on to life with the slimmest of a thread. He motioned the woman to enter a small alley off Massachusetts Avenue. John blocked the alley so no one could peer in.

Winston smiled at the mom. She stared at him with big eyes, gazing deep into his blue eyes, as if she could see his past, and the depths of his soul and being. A calmness overcame her. John felt the calmness, too. The child moved for the first time. He opened one eye, and then the other. Winston left the gaze of the woman and looked at the boy. He smiled, and boy smiled back, his first smile in months. Winston grabbed the boy's two hands and bent over and whispered something into the boy's ear. He then placed his hand on the boy's forehead. The mom shifted her gaze to her son. John looked on as well. He loved to look at the white light. The white light shined again. The boy took a huge breath, and then another. He jumped down from his mother's embrace and stood. He shook one leg, and then the other. He raised one arm, and then the other. He jumped once, and then again. He started to dance. He was a good dancer. Finally, he belted out a yell of joy that pierced through the air of the small alley. Up above, a Grandmother waved her hands up and down.

"God bless you!" She shouted.

John put his index finger over his lips.

"Our secret," his lips said.

The Grandmother winked.

The boy slapped Winston on the back. He ran to the street as fast as he could. His mom chased him in utter, thrilling joy. John smiled at Winston. Winston just nodded.

It was now noon. Jackhammer had two more hours.

"Where to now?" John asked.

"Onward!"

And with that Winston walked briskly down Massachusetts Avenue the other way towards the Back Bay.

Meanwhile, the former blind man was spotted by some of his cohorts.

One shouted for all to hear.

"You are no longer blind! Paul, you are no longer blind!"

"Praise to the Lord! Long Live the King! Hail to the Angel! The aliens are setting a trap! Santa and the elf did this!"

No one knew for sure.

6.

INSTON TOOK A SHARP TURN. He ran down the steps to the subway system on the green line. He was cold. It was a bit warmer underground. He walked to a map of the subway system. He wondered where to go next. He knew his final destination-the hospital. But that had to be at dusk. He was not sure why, just a feeling. He pulled out his smart phone. He put on his earplugs and sat on a bench. He saw dozens of people run by him up the steps, shouting, yelling.

"Hosanna in the highest!" he thought he heard.

He turned on THE radio talk show. He wanted to unwind a little, and listen to Jackhammer, who made him laugh.

He heard Jackhammer.

"A man, an alien, an angel, or Santa, or an Elf, or the Messiah, or a prophet, or a King, who knows! Some people have been healed. John the Baptist said he was healed. Four other callers have called and said they were healed. Do you believe in miracles on Massachusetts Avenue? I could be saying this for ratings. And if so, isn't it great just to think that something like this could happen on a quiet day in the middle of the holiday week, when so many are at home, not in the city, or down in a sunny climate, or skiing up north or out west. Or visiting relatives in Minnesota or Chicago or Syracuse.

"Or if it is true! Stay tuned to the Jackhammer show. We are the only show covering this spectacle, the miracles on, no, the Massachusetts Avenue miracles. Yes, the Massachusetts Avenue miracles. Where are my callers? My witnesses. Who is the healer? Is this The Awakening? Or a Martian attack? Can we now forever say that there really is a Santa? Or there is an angel sent from heaven! Or God is sending his messenger? Or a King from the ancient past has returned. Or is he a prophet setting the stage? Is Armageddon coming? Again, is this The Awakening? Is the Holy Spirit among us? Am I insane? I want to believe. I saw the white light! My sister, ah, nothing."

Winston felt the gravity of his actions. Unlike London, his actions were setting fire to the emotions and souls of the people on Massachusetts Avenue. And with the most popular talk radio show host on board, the conflagration might ignite into a raging storm.

Maybe I should stop now. Many are healed. Enough for one day. Anonymity may be soon lost forever. An avalanche of people will be on my doorstep to be healed. I don't have the power or ability to heal all. The reservoir is deep but not limitless. I don't know. He took off his earplugs. He maybe had heard enough. He saw the map. He could take a couple subway trains to south station, and board a rail car back to Connecticut and stop all of this?

As he turned off his earplugs, he heard a young woman shout at the top of her lungs.

"A blind man has been healed! He can see! A woman's dead son was raised from the dead! Hosanna in the highest! Alleluia! Praise be to the Lord! Lord have mercy! Where is the healer? I need to see the healer!"

Winston watched as the young woman then buckled over and collapsed. Others rushed past her. Many stepped on her to join the chorus above on the streets. Winston feared she might be trampled to death. The story of the blind man and the mother and her boy had spread so quickly. He wondered how the story of a dead boy had evolved. *The boy was alive. I saw the thread of his life. What was the mother telling people? Maybe she thought he had died. I cannot bring someone back to life. I am not the Messiah. Maybe I should call Jackhammer. NO. NO. Not now.*

The subway car had emptied. Winston saw the young woman in a heap. She must have been alone. No friends were coming back to get her. She wore a local college sweatshirt. *Must be a college student who didn't go home.* He saw a cord of life, more than a thread. But her face was smashed in. Her nose flattened. Her right eye appeared dislodged. She was knocked unconscious. Her jubilation turned to tragedy. *And it is my fault.*

Certainly, there were cameras everywhere. His image would be bounced around the world for all to see. But she was severely injured. Permanently scarred and damaged. He heard another car approaching. *More people that will trample her.* He walked over, picked her up, and threw her over his shoulder. He carried her up the steps. It was not far. Eventually, he returned to the alley. John was not there to run interference. But people were flocking to the other end of Massachusetts Avenue towards Interstate 93, where his first healings had occurred. Where the blind man now was. Where the child raised from the dead was. *NOT TRUE.*

He entered the alley. There was the Grandmother. She put a finger over her lips. *My lips are sealed.* He lay the college young woman down. The cord of life was getting thinner. Her breaths shallower. He now saw her left ear was gone. Blood was oozing out, taking her life away, slowly. He wondered why she so desperately wanted to see the healer. Was there something else? He soon saw blackness throughout her body. She was riddled with cancer. She had come to be healed. Maybe she had left a hospital. Maybe she was not at home because she was in a hospital, or a hospice. He did not know.

Winston looked up and saw the Grandmother. She was weeping. *What are you waiting for?*

Winston held the young woman to his chest. He whispered into her good ear. He put his hand over her back. He could see the white light. The Grandmother could see the white light. He hoped none of the throng walking by would see the white light.

Soon the young woman awoke. He could see her ear was back. Her eye was back in its socket. Her face was reformed, and actually more beautiful than before. A radiance filled her face. The blackness dissipated into the air. Winston waved his hand over the blackness and erased it from the air. The Grandmother fainted, seeing the miracle in such vivid detail.

The young woman looked deeply into Winston's blue eyes. She was calm and serene.

"I saw you in my dreams. I saw white clouds, and a bright blue sky. I saw a monumental Temple and a Palace, and large behemoth rock formations jutting from the ocean floor. Was that Atlantis? Heaven? I saw the white light last night. I saw the videos of Santa and the elf. I saw the letters inscribed on the snow on the Charles River. I knew you would heal me and save me! I will keep our secret of who you are! Long live the King!"

"What is your name?"

"Becca."

"Oh, I know a Becca from London. Very important person in my life."

"Of course. Thank you so much! My parents are on their way from Oklahoma to watch me die. Now, they will see me alive and reborn. Awakened! Is that the case?"

"Yes, that is what I have heard. I need to go. So, long."

Winston brushed back his hair. He suddenly realized he had brushed back his hair. But he did not have much hair, other than a comb over.

"Your hair is long! And silvery white! You look like a King. Was it not long before today?"

"No, it was not. And in London, well, you don't know about London. My hair did not grow. Hmm. Amazing. Not sure about this. I need a hat. No white light in London, either."

Winston found his Patriots pullover cap. He put it over his flowing locks. He left the alley.

The young woman saw the Grandmother. She found her way up to her apartment. She sat down for a warm cup of coffee.

Who is this Becca from London?

7.

W INSTON WENT BACK TO THE SUBWAY. He looked up at the camera. He saw it was out of order. No videos to go viral. At least not for now. He did not see any on the way back from the alley either. He took a big breath. Soon another phalanx of people marched up the stairs. *In search of healing. But I cannot heal all.*

The mother with her now healthy son had decided to grab the attention. She broke her vow of silence and confidentiality. She exaggerated his healing by saying her son had been dead.

"I was in the alley! The holy alley! The alley to a parallel universe! A wormhole! The path to Atlantis! Or the highway to heaven! The Lord is coming! From the Portal in the alley! Hosanna in the highest!" She had yelled and collapsed, as the throng gasped.

"On to the alley! To the Portal! To the Lord! To heaven!"

Madness swept the streets. Dozens swooned and fell limp to the ground, as others walked over them, rushing to the Portal to heaven. Many shrieked hysterically, calling for forgiveness. Others just marveled at the sudden crowd hysteria.

Hundreds soon gathered by the alley. Many ran down the alley trying to enter the Portal. But they just kept going to a parallel street. They could not return as hundreds followed them. Those on Massachusetts Avenue screamed that hundreds had entered the Portal and were in heaven. Or another universe, or Atlantis, or an alien ship or world, or Mars, or even China.

The crowd pressed forward even faster. The Grandmother kept yelling that there was no Portal.

Finally, Becca, now down at the entrance to the alley, grabbed a megaphone from a nearby construction site.

"The healer is gone. He walked through the Portal and closed it behind him. He will come again next decade, the day after Christmas, like this year. You should all go home. There is no residual energy or force or healing power. He may be a messenger of the Lord, or a King, or an alien or an angel. But he is gone. Let us be blessed for those that he did heal!" Becca gasped, doing her best, even though with dishonesty, to preserve the safety and secrecy of her healer.

Soon many had returned from a loop around the block. They shouted that they had not gone through a Portal. The crowd simmered. It started to disperse. Dozens stayed to pray and thank the Lord for his healing through the healer. Others laughed at the spectacle, saying no one was even healed. The mother of the supposedly risen son, looked disheveled and poor. Many soon disparaged her and discredited her story.

Anger mounted for some. They turned their anger to Jackhammer for bringing false hope to the people. His lines lit up with disdainful callers, but believing and thankful callers called in as well.

Winston turned his earplugs back on to hear the streaming of the radio station from his smartphone.

"Jackhammer, you sure got your ratings! But dozens were trampled by the throngs trying to get to the wormhole or

Portal. And it doesn't exist! Their blood is on your shoulders!"

"Jackhammer! You stirred our collective consciousness to a spiritual high! Healing did occur. But the healer is gone. He left through the alley back to his spiritual kingdom! But I felt his presence! I am transformed! I am Awakened! God bless mankind. God save us!"

"Jackhammer! The healer is gone! Back through the Portal. Must have been the white light that you saw last night, when he first came through the Portal. A magical being. I think he was an angel. Not the Lord. The healer will come back in ten years, like the girl said. Maybe the Lord will come, too. We have ten years to repent and be worthy. Thank you for letting Boston know about the angel!"

"Jackhammer! You did it again. A complete fairy tale bought by the masses. Your highest rating ever, and on the quietest of days. Yes, another raise coming your way!"

"Jackhammer, did he really leave. I am so sad. This is Anna."

Jackhammer just listened to his callers. Hundreds of thousands were listening not only in Boston, but all across the country on live streaming. Even other parts of the world were catching up to the news, or fake news, of the Massachusetts Avenue miracles.

Two o'clock had not come soon enough. Jackhammer signed off.

Jackhammer hugged Sandy. She shivered. She liked him. They both were single, he a few years older.

"I have to see my sister. I have to call Anna. I have to piece this together. Honestly, I believe there was a healer. Too bad he left before Anna could be healed. And I wanted to thank him for healing my sister. I am shaken by this. Tomorrow folks will want to know if this was a Jackhammer fable or Jackhammer's bible. I have to investigate."

Jackhammer hung his broad shoulders lower, as he held the weight of the public uproar on them.

"I don't think he left through any Portal. I think someone, that young woman, was simply protecting him. Certainly, a Portal is not believable. But then again healing is not believable either, except for those with faith, or belief in their Lord or Savior, or God. I think he is still in Boston. I think he is a man, and not an angel. I feel his presence. But he is special, for sure," Sandy smiled, looking intelligent and thoughtful and at peace.

"I think that Santa and the elf know something. They were not too far from where my sister was healed, miraculously. A white light. I must find them. I am heading out that way now. Want to join me!" He smiled for the first time in hours.

"Perhaps. Maybe."

He looked away.

"Definitely, wait up!"

He fist-pumped her. She thought that odd but responded. She was once an athlete, too. It was after 2 p.m.

The Boston police cordoned off the alley of the alleged Portal on both sides. Massachusetts Avenue was on lock down. No cars or other vehicles were allowed. Pedestrians were forced to go another way. Only residents and business owners, and the homeless who held court daily, were allowed to stay.

The FBI soon showed up. They were in the Grandmother's house. They grilled her. But she kept her composure. Memories of the large man putting a finger over his lips kept her firm. The young woman had left. The FBI wanted to question her. They issued an APB to find her. Soon, the National Guard arrived. The President of the United States wanted a full investigation. An alien force was not a welcome idea. Nor was the thought of an advanced society that could enter our earth through a Portal. And if the messenger of the Lord or an angel, were here, he wanted to know. He also wanted to be healed of his undisclosed ailments, none fatal, but so painful and bothersome. Everyone wanted to be healed. Everyone wanted to believe. Secretly, he made plans to go to Boston.

But there was no APB for Winston, because no one knew he was the healer. No one knew what he looked like. The blind man feigned to be blind again when the police found him.

"The story is bogus after all," one investigator lamented, holding his sore back.

Those who had been trampled, none terribly, were taken care of. All were released from arca hospitals.

Winston knew his ultimate game plan. Healing the homeless on Massachusetts Avenue was not planned. It just happened. People were in the right place at the right time, on his morning walk.

Winston hopped on the subway and headed to Quincy Market. St. Aloysius Hospital was on his mind.

8.

WINSTON ARRIVED AT THE GOVERNMENT CENTER STOP ON THE GREEN LINE. He took a few steps down from the subway car onto the pavement. There were few people around. This was in the financial district. Many did not work this week. No one paid any attention to him. Everyone on the platform was one with their smartphones. The smartphones were part of their being, part of their mind, part of their entire existence. Man was evolving, he thought, into part man, and part computer, or artificial intelligence. Intelligence was evolving on its own, but it was still inextricably linked to the mind of man, a new symbiosis. Would man and artificial intelligence evolve into a new evolutionary juggernaut! Would intelligence ever separate from man and evolve independently of man, and his body. In competition with man? Even the body would evolve, more and more linked to robotics and biometrics.

He wondered how his healing power was linked in. He was not aware of any artificial intelligence that could heal. He recalled in London his memories of an ancient continent. The lost continent. Atlantis. That he had been a King. That was his vision. And that there were crystals from the ancient continent that provided access to a healing force.

That he had regained access to higher spiritual realms. That in those realms, he could access healing powers from the crystals. Was that true? Or, was that a vision his mind came up with for him to assuage his fears that the healing was deeper, or mystical, or spiritual, or from God, or the Lord. In London, he fully subscribed to the theory of Atlantis, and his past as its King. His visions of Atlantis were so clear. The pillars in the ocean, the Temple, the Palace, the healing fountains, the tall Atlanteans, with flowing white robes; the final catastrophic destruction of the continent. He recalled the wireless energy, and wireless communication, and wireless healing energy. But was the vision true?

Were the American pundits, cynics and critics, right? Was he an alien, or prophet, or messenger from God? Was he from a parallel universe? Or Santa?

It did not matter. And then he heard a booming voice.

"He came through the Portal! The Portal is closed! It is not accessible or visible! The police have cordoned off the whole area around the Massachusetts Avenue miracles. The healer is gone!" A man, who looked like he made the subway is home, belted out. The man then buckled to his knees.

"I missed the Messiah! I hope he comes back for me!" Winston yelled back.

"He is not the Messiah, he is a King from another time and space!"

The homeless man was startled.

"But the Messiah is a King. He is from another time and space. God bless me! I want to go to the kingdom of heaven!"

The homeless man was overwhelmed with emotion and collapsed to the floor. Winston saw his life fully tethered to his body. *He is fine. Too many cameras around.* Winston left to go up the escalator, back to the frigid cold air. But he looked back and saw a darkness in the man's body trunk. The man was dying, unknown to the man. Winston casually walked over to him. He whispered into his ear. He put his hand underneath his coat to block the white light, and he healed the man of his dark, evil disease. He left quickly before the man awoke. Up the escalator he strode.

As he left through the glass doors to the brick paved government center, he heard the man bellow.

"I have been saved! I have been saved! Blessed be the Lord!" He heard a thump. The man had fainted again.

Winston covered his face with the lapel on his black overcoat. It was indeed cold. He was not sure what he was going to do next. Jackhammer was no longer on the radio. He jaunted over to the Faneuil Hall area. He crossed Congress Street, and soon entered one of the market buildings. He grabbed a peanut butter chocolate chip cookie and a cup of hot coffee and sat down on a wooden stool in the sitting area in the center of the building.

He watched as dozens of tourists, visitors, and some working people walked by. Most were paired with their smartphones, but some talked with their friends. When he finished his cookie, he took his cup of coffee with him and headed out to the end of the building There was a crowd of people huddled around a bar. A television was on. He peered through to the television.

There was Massachusetts Avenue. Reporters were everywhere. A television reporter was explaining how there was a Portal to another parallel universe, another part of our universe, Atlantis, or heaven! He was not sure which. That the healer was gone. And that healer had closed the Portal. A woman claiming to have met the healer stated that he would be back in ten years minus a day. That mankind needed to be prepared for his return. Or the return of the Messiah himself!

Images of people praying and chanting from different parts of the city were aired. A lead Christian leader confirmed that the healer was sent by the Lord, that he was a messenger and prophet for the Lord, and an angel. That The Awakening had begun. That the Holy Spirit was about to infuse Boston. It was to begin in Boston as foretold by visionaries. And it was happening now.

Just then there was an aerial of the Charles River, where Santa and the elf had been seen. Carved into the frozen river snow was the phrase THE AWAKENING.

The Christian leader boldly proclaimed it was a message from the Lord.

Winston watched, as many in the crowd scoffed at the reports, but saw others roar in approval. Still others wailed for salvation and praised the Lord.

One little girl said she always knew Santa was real. Now, she knew where he came from. Through a Portal on an alley off of Massachusetts Avenue in the South End area of Boston.

"No wonder the Boston sports teams always win. The Portal to heaven is in Boston!" A Bostonian cheered.

Winston slipped away. He walked across Atlantic Avenue.

So, everyone thinks I have left for ten years. Maybe I should just go home to Connecticut. The Messiah, I am not. Maybe the Christion leader is correct. Maybe I am an angel or messenger of the Lord. I don't know. But I can heal people. Whether it is Atlantean technology and spiritual power, or the power of the Lord, does it matter? And is Atlantean spiritual power one in the same with the power of the Lord. Did the Lord live in Atlantis?

I am from Atlantis. I was its former King. The Lord and God are real. Maybe it all ties together. Some Atlanteans could traverse with their souls to higher spiritual realms. Maybe the Lord dwelled in the highest spiritual realm. I recall the Universal Force. God and the Universal Force, one in the same? And certainly, forces from above want salvation for mankind.

And technology and its evolution may be a way to reach the higher realms of existence, possibly. With technology, all of man may someday be connected, as if there is one giant mind with so many points of access. Like a giant blockchain, but with human minds as the points. Man may build a path to God with the aid of technology. The spiritual realms may have a scientific basis in quantum physics. Science and religion may evolve together to reach nirvana. As man and technology grow together. Maybe the Atlanteans had all of this figured out. But dark forces wanted to stop it. Maybe the archfiend of all time wanted to stop man and technology and the advancement to God and the Universal Force. Or maybe the spiritual realms and God are not scientific. I do not know. But I believe in my healing powers. I believe in God and Universal Force, and the higher spiritual realms, and Atlantis!

But today. I can only focus on healing. I may not have another day with my healing powers. I have not healed anyone since London. I must heal those in need. If my cover is blown, so be it.

Winston reached the waterfront. This part of Boston was relatively quiet. He looked across to the airport. The planes took off and landed. The ice flows in Boston Harbor seemed to frolic and play. He saw a movement near a pier. He walked to the movement.

There he saw a homeless little girl. She was nearly frozen to death. He saw her cord of life was weathered and thin. He pulled her out from underneath the pier. He whispered into her ear and put his hand on her heart. He saw the white light. The little girl beamed in joy.

"I prayed that the healer would find me. You found me. I will keep your secret. I came back here to die. I heard the healer left through the Portal to go back home. I think to Atlantis. And heaven."

"Ah, little girl. What you say is what I believe. But it is our secret. Here is a gift card I received from my friend who I healed in Connecticut. It is $200. Go buy a warm coat and go to the homeless shelter. Have them call the State social services to find you a foster home."

A man tapped Winston on the shoulder. He was weeping. His wife was next to him. She was weeping. They were warmly and impeccably dressed. They looked like they were of extreme substance and importance. But now they were meek.

"We saw what you did. We saw the white light. We believe. We praise the Lord every day. We want to serve the Lord. We will take her in as our foster child. We will let the state know. We will provide for her and place her into the best private schools. Praise to the Lord. When you go back to heaven, or Atlantis, or the parallel universe, or alien planet, tell the Lord we will wait for his return in ten years. God bless you, the healer, messenger, angel of God!"

The girl hugged Winston and ran into the open arms of her new foster parents. Winston guessed she was eight years old. She was of mixed descent, and he felt she was an orphan.

"You are right," she said to him.

Off the new family went. Winston smiled. He remembered the orphan boy from London, who ended up with a caretaker Mum. He fondly remembered his time in London. And the joyous and wonderful ball with the Queen. And he still read Becca's column every day. His daughter still lived there. She had not inherited his healing powers. But maybe that was ok.

Winston saw dusk was not too far off.

Suddenly, two men were upon him. He did not know if they would harm him or rob him. He only had his wallet and smartphone.

"You are the healer! You healed us on the Charles River near the boathouse. We left our wheel chairs there. No one has put it together that we were Santa and the elf. But they may. We are the ones that carved THE AWAKENING into the snow-covered river. We are both Christians, and when you healed us, we were certain The Awakening had begun. We do not believe you are the Lord, or the Messiah, but that he sent you. And now, in modern times, maybe we understand more on how the Lord operates. That he sent you here through the Portal. We saw the white light in the sky before you healed the young woman and us. We suspected it was you coming through the Portal, or the light was sent from the Lord to you through the Portal. Or maybe the light was the Holy Spirit. We knew the Portal is not on Massachusetts Avenue, but somewhere near the Charles River and the boathouse. We suspected you were still in Boston. We are highly attuned to your presence, because you healed us. We were drawn here by your presence. Maybe, your powers. And we saw you heal the girl, and secretly heal her two new foster parents. We can see now, what we could not before. The foster mother was dying and did not know it, and the foster father, was close to a coronary, and did not know it. We saw the darkness dissipate. You are truly holy, and an angel! The man stopped talking, and sank to his knees, as did the smaller man next to him.

"So, where did you get those costumes?"

The smaller man raised his head, at first reverently, and then casually.

"We attended a costume party on Christmas Eve. I was an elf. He was Santa. Thursday night after you healed us, we went back home and put on our costumes. We still have the costumes at home."

"How were you disabled?"

"We both were injured on a tour of duty for our country!"

"Glad to serve you back, young men! Go now and serve the common good."

"We thought with our military training, we could be your body guards, and escort. That would serve the common good and enable us to pay you back!" Santa exhorted him.

"Indeed, we march as three now. There is a place I want to go. It is where I wanted to go last night. Follow me."

"No, follow us first. We will keep this discreet, but we have four combat friends in need of healing. They are not far from here, in a soldier's home. Then you will have six body guards."

"And so, it shall be. Lead me there. But don't say I need twelve body guards. You know, apostles. You are not apostles, and I am not the Lord! A King, alien, messenger, prophet, alien, angel, maybe. Got it!"

"Just testing. I like you as a King."

"Yes, I think I was the King of Atlantis. Not sure where in the time-space continuum Atlantis may be, or if it is in a parallel universe, or part of our universe accessible through the Portal! Or actually, part of our world history, as told by Plato! But there, the high priests had extraordinary healing powers. Whether it was from the spiritual realms or from power crystals, or both, I am not sure. Somehow, I believe the crystals are still on earth, and I have the power from the higher spiritual realms to access them to heal. Or my power and the white light comes from the Holy Spirit who I believe came through the Portal last night. The higher realms, or heaven, indeed may be accessible through the Portal. I have healed before in London. You see, I know I have the power to heal, but I am not fully aware of why and where. But if you think of me as King or an angel, or that I too came through the Portal, I am fine with that. On to your friends!"

"Did you heal anyone else, after you left Massachusetts Avenue?"

"Why?" Winston looked concerned, as he folded his arms across his chest.

"There is a bulletin that dozens of people at a bar in Quincy Market were healed of all their infirmities and ailments, large and small. They all claimed they saw a white light and felt an enormous presence. It is all over the newswires. The Portal must not have been closed after all!"

"My, it worked. I saw all the people. Most were silently praying to be healed. I saw all of them had dark spots of varying degrees. I said I will heal all of them. That they likely would not know I healed them until later. It looks like it worked. Maybe I am an angel after all."

The elf spoke up. "We believe in you."

Winston smiled at the elf and Santa. "For this journey, I shall call you the elf, and you Santa, just as you were on the river. Those shall be your names. Let's now find your friends and heal more along the way. The white light inside me is growing so powerful by the moment. Onward!"

9.

J ACKHAMMER HUNG UP THE SMARTPHONE. His sister was still in shock, that she had been saved. She had been so lost in thought. She did not notice how close she was to Storrow Drive, until it was too late, and she heard the splat of her body against the car. She was studying for her doctorate in physics at a local university and had been so close to a breakthrough on some higher-level equations on the existence of a multiverse. She saw her body in the street, as she felt herself drifting away. She saw the thread of life, about to break, then a white light. An elder gentleman whispered into her ear. He put his hand on her heart. She plunged back into her body. Gawkers stared at her. Two paramedics awkwardly stood by as she stood with torn blood-stained clothes. She told them she was fine. They left her at a coffee shop. She called her brother in a panic. He invited her to his condominium in the Seaport.

But his sister talked of the multiverse on this call. That a Portal was mathematically possible. That advances in technology could exist where a visitor could use an energy source to heal. She was convinced she was healed as proof of the multiverse. Whether the healer was an angel or an alien, or a messenger from God did not matter. Were they not one in the same? She had called her friend and protégé,

Becca, that morning, to tell her about the healer, on listening to her brother build up the Massachusetts Avenue miracles. Becca, near death, left for the South End, not waiting for her parents. His sister later told him that Becca was healed. The healer had healed her. There was some talk of Atlantis. His sister, again, thought that whatever the other side was called did not matter. The multiverse and Portals had the backing of mathematics. *I will seek out the healer to explore these possibilities! I will find Becca to join me.*

It was approaching dusk. Breaking news of the healing at Quincy Market was exploding on social media. His radio station had called him. The station wanted him to come to their downtown station, near North Station, and marshal the news of the healer. And where was Sandy? They wanted her, too.

Jackhammer stared at Sandy. They had fallen in love in an instant, among all the hysteria and joy. He had proposed to her on the spot, and she accepted. A romantic interlude at the possible the end of the world?

"Let's find the healer and have him marry us!" Sandy suggested, with only a slight hope of such a result in her face. They had gone to Massachusetts Avenue to no avail. They ended up at a coffee shop in the Back Bay, watching their smartphones.

"The station wants us to come back in to report on the healer's journey throughout the city. People are turning to our station first for news on the healer. The station doesn't want to drop that advantage. Let's go. Maybe later the healer will know we are his biggest fans, and he will marry us! Doubt it, but who knows!"

"Let's go now. How crowded is the city? Can we get downtown with a cab?"

"They said if we leave now, we can make it in. The access highways to Boston are backing up like a morning commute. It will be packed soon. If the healer is discovered, he could be in physical jeopardy. That is probably why he wants secrecy and anonymity. I hope he survives, or leaves quickly through the Portal," Jackhammer brushed back his dark brown hair out of his green colored eyes in concern.

"Let's go. Nobody knows what we look like, we are on the radio!"

Winston, Santa and the elf slipped through the growing throngs with calmness and anonymity for now. They soon reached a soldier's home near North Station and near the Charles River where their friends were in rehab. The four were eagerly waiting, fully believing that The Awakening was in full gear.

Winston smiled at the four young men, two African Americans, one Cuban American and one Boston Irishman. He thanked them for their service and whispered into their ears. Soon a white light enveloped them, and they were fully healed.

"HooRah!" They whooped and hollered and hugged each other in joy. Winston raised his hand.

"We have a mission to complete. You shall protect me from the crowds, particularly, if they think I am the healer. You must deny it. Let's march on. I may heal along the way. You are my eyes and ears. Let's go men. But don't use any weapons."

Winston looked at them, as they one by one removed their weapons. They nodded their heads, and off they went.

Winston saw an elder woman, the nurse at the home. He walked over to her. He whispered into her ears and brushed her hair with his hand. A white light enveloped her head. Gone was her early stage dementia. Her gray hair was now blonde, her figure years younger. Decades younger. She gasped in joy and fell to her knees to pray. One of the soldiers looked back and wondered who the beautiful woman was kneeling on the floor.

Jackhammer arrived at the station. He grabbed the mike and was ready to rock.

"The healer has not left us! He did not go back through the Portal. The Portal is not on Massachusetts Avenue. I have reason to believe it is near the Charles River in the Back Bay, close to Kenmore Square. I may share that reason later. I have reason to believe two other visitors may have come through the Portal with the healer. Not sure though. They are dressed as Santa and an elf. Maybe they are healers. Or they are his guards. Or maybe they were healed by the healer and did not come through the Portal. You remember them. They made the news last night. I believe that is not a coincidence that they were on the ice last night. And I believe, but have not confirmed, they were the ones that inscribed THE AWAKENING on the snow-covered ice."

Jackhammer was perspiring profusely and breathing heavily. Sandy brought him some more news. A plane full of celebrities was flying in from Los Angeles. They were looking for a fountain of youth. Their vanity was exhausting, and sickening, but the hysteria was on.

Jackhammer ranted on about the multiverse, Portals, and parallel universes. He spoke of science and religion. He rambled. The stories were rehashed again and again.

Mobs of people flooded the Back Bay on Beacon Street and Commonwealth Avenue. Praying, singing and chanting was piercing the air. His sister had called. She was going to the Back Bay, too, to find the healer. She hoped to find Becca first.

"Anna is on the line," Sandy excitedly blurted out, her blue eyes dazzling in the office light. "Do you want it as a private call?"

"Yes!"

Jackhammer took a big breath.

"Hi Anna. He is back. Are you ready?"

"I am, but will he know we are here. How does he know who we even are? There are ten of us up here. And many more below. We are all days or hours away from our deaths," Anna sniffled, worrying this great event would pass her and her friends by.

"Maybe death is not so bad. Maybe all this proves there is life after death, or life elsewhere in the universe or multi-verse. My sister said she was alive, as she drifted away from her body. She felt her soul or spirit was not killed by the car. She saw the thread of life, hanging on. Maybe if the thread broke her spirit would have gone, too, but she is convinced it was separate being."

Sandy glared at Jackhammer.

"AH, you want to live! My sister is looking for the healer. She thinks she knows what the healer looks like. I will call her and tell her about you and your friends. She should find the healer. I am sure he is on his way back to his Portal. Maybe they can catch him before he leaves," Jackhammer said compassionately with the assent of Sandy.

"Thank you so much! I love you so much! I have to go. I am tired and out of breath," Anna drifted off into a subconscious state. Her smartphone dropped to the ground.

A nurse walked in and shut off the phone. She tucked Anna under the covers, and gently brushed her hair back with her hand. She hooked up her IVs with nourishment and painkillers.

"Poor child! If only the healer would stop here before he goes back home."

Jackhammer's voice belted out over the airwaves and internet.

"BREAKING NEWS! Again, incredible breaking news. The Cardinal of the Catholic Church has issued a proclamation that all of his flock should go to church to pray. He believes that the healer may in fact be a messenger from the Lord. He used the words The Awakening!"

Jackhammer could not say anymore. He wondered where his sister was. He wondered if the healer would survive. He wondered if the healer might reach Anna and her friends. How would Boston survive The Awakening? What would the rest of the world think? Would this all end up as a big ruse, or an event that happened, but that was not provable? Would the pundits, heretics, and atheists scoff? Would the religious leaders revert and say it was all a misunderstanding? Would it be the scientists, like his sister, who pushed the mantra that the healings did occur? Where would all this end up? And if the healer left, what would be left of The Awakening?

Sandy was lost in thought, too. All the lines were full. She just stared at the blinking lights. Jackhammer called his sister and told her about Anna.

10.

ECCA ARRIVED at Beacon Street near Kenmore Square. Thousands were gathered around the square, many holding candles. She had taken the subway, and was searching for her friend and mentor at school, Savannah Jackson, Jackhammer's sister. Savannah had called and told her the story of the miracle on Storrow Drive. Hearing the story had saved Becca's life. It confirmed her dream of Atlantis or heaven. She had immediately left her hospice to find the healer. And it was fortuitous that she had been trampled, as the healer was miraculously there to find her. She was religious and thanked the Lord. But she thought of Atlantis and its King. *What is the connection?* Becca and Savannah talked again about her miracle at the subway station, and then about Anna. Becca wanted to help. *I have to find the healer to heal Anna before he leaves through the Portal for his parallel universe, or heaven, or spiritual realm, or Atlantis! I want to thank him, again, too!*

Becca bumped her way through the undulating crowd. She prayed with those who prayed and sung with those who sung. She had seen a glimpse of herself in a mirror. She was startled at her healthy and glowing appearance. She thought she had seen a halo around her head, or a white light. A remnant from her healing perhaps. And her hair was lustrous and full and long. *How could my hair be long again so quickly? My parent's will not recognize me.* Her parents had arrived at Boston. They did not go to her hospice. They were somewhere in the crowds, drawn into the magnitude of the happenings. They were Midwestern Christians and felt blessed at the timing of their visit to Boston. And Becca had told them she had been healed by the healer himself. Her mother was ill from diabetes and arthritis, her father recovering from prostate cancer. Maybe they could be healed from the aura of the crowd. Maybe the crowd itself could generate healing energies, drawing from the healer himself. Becca saw light brown hair falling down her shoulders across her coat. It seemed to be growing as she walked. She took off her hat and tied her hair into a bun, and tucked it under her pullover cap. She headed down Beacon Street towards Dartmouth Street to find Savannah.

Savannah was on Beacon Street, near Dartmouth Street. She waited for Becca, as the stream of people grew. Savannah even thought maybe she would be able to recognize the healer.

It was 5:00 P.M. Jackhammer and Sandy were still at the radio station. It was past dusk. Most of the other radio stations went off air. The television stations and numerous social media outlets had taken over the story. Reporters and their crews were on most corners on Commonwealth Avenue and Beacon Street. But many people still streamed Jackhammer for updates. But Jackhammer did not have feet on the ground other than his sister, and eventually, Becca. He was getting newsfeeds off the wires, social media and the television reports. Nonetheless, he had started the story, and was inextricably linked to the story and the healer by the masses of his listeners, including those outside of Boston in the suburbs, and across the nation. Many streamed his audio live, while watching their television sets, or smartphones, computers and tablets for video.

Winston and his gang of six marched along the sidewalk running parallel to the Charles River and Storrow Drive, where many Bostonians jogged for their daily exercise during the better weather months. He looked out at the river, so white with a perfect blanket of snow. Many marched with them, not knowing he was the healer. Santa and the elf were without costume and blended in with the marchers.

"Are you heading back to your Portal? Are you taking any of us with you?" One of the soldiers asked, running to the front to walk alongside Winston. His chest was pumped up now, as his body was military grade again from the healing. The soldier felt so invigorated and healthy. He had shouted for joy every thirty seconds until finally Santa gave him a big hug and told him not to draw attention to the healer and himself. His hair had grown a bit longer, too, and he yearned for a short military style haircut. I am looking like an angel, he thought to himself, as he looked at the silvery hair flowing down the shoulders of the healer. His name was Jose. He had saved eight soldiers in Afghanistan, with heroic valor. He had lost both legs in the ensuing melee. Now his legs were back, adorned with powerful muscles, and bronzed skin. He was so thankful. He bellowed a loud yell again. Hoorah! Other marchers just bellowed out with him. Santa let it go.

"I will not bring anyone with me through the Portal," exclaimed Winston. Winston then drifted into his thoughts from earlier.

The Portal. It exists, I am sure, and I will see it. After all, I do have these healing powers. And they come from somewhere. In London, I was certain they came from Atlantis, from the higher spiritual realms tied to the Atlantean crystals still on earth. But now, I see, it may be the Lord, through the Holy Spirit, who is acting through me to heal, to commence The Awakening.

This is The Awakening. Maybe others will discover they have the power within to help others or the common good. The power of the collective prayers, chants, screams, bellows, joy and happiness might raise and elevate the souls of all around me in Boston, to achieve remarkable heights, and remarkable joy and cheer. And freedom from the bondages of mental and physical pain and suffering. The Awakening. It is happening. I am a catalyst. I am a messenger. The healing in London was a test, an experiment. It worked. Many were healed. Those that were healed remained silent, until the Royal Ball, but those at the ball were discreet as well. There was no international sensationalist reporting. London was not flooded with youth seeking wealthy elders, or the desperately ill. I was left alone. Even my few friends who were healed kept silent. It is if a guiding force kept them all at bay. It was not the time for The Awakening. Now it is time for The Awakening to begin. This is boundless. This is miraculous. Freedom may indeed arise for all the souls of mankind.

I believe The Awakening is a glimpse. A glimpse of how things can be, if mankind finds his God, his Lord, the Holy Spirit, the Universal Force, or inner spiritual self. A unison of all religious beliefs. A bonding with the Almighty, the Creator, the Universal Force. An ascension into heaven, or the higher spiritual realms. I do not know. But I feel the enormous energy. The love and grace emanating from a higher source. Is it funneling through this Portal for today only? Is the Portal the path to the Lord, heaven or Atlantis, or another universe? Does every individual have access to the Portal, or their own Portal, or is it a universal entrance? And then there is technology and science, that I thought of earlier, and its connection to Portals, and spiritual realms, and the Universal Force.

I can see the spirits of the marchers. The spirits are on fire. The white light of their souls is glowing. Love is flowing rampantly. Strangers are helping each other. There is a march to Kenmore

Square and beyond. They all want to see the Portal. Many want and need to be healed. There are actors and actresses that want to be young again. Some older athletes are dreaming of the glory days. Not all want to be healed for the right reasons. But most are here because they feel the energy of The Awakening. The force of the Holy Spirit or Universal Force. The love of all souls. The goodness that is in the hearts of all men and women. The core of everyone's good side. The Awakening. The drowning the negative energies of self-adornment and greed and selfishness and the dark forces of evil and debauchery. The population is lifting.

"Healer! You are lost in thought. The marching has stopped. There is no place to go. As far as we can see, there are marchers. We are even with Hereford Street. It is not that much further to Kenmore Square. I can see thousands of candles flickering. What do you want to do next? Is there going to be some sort of mass healing?" the elf spoke up, for the first time on the relentless march.

"There is a place I want to go to, first, before I head home," Winston mumbled back. He shook as he watched all the candles flickering.

"My internal energy is combustible. It could explode to the skies. It could happen. The energy is building to a crescendo. Maybe all that are near me from here on shall be healed. Or maybe more. Maybe all. I shall let the white light do its bountiful work. Those that are healthy will feel youthful and energetic. Those in need of healing shall be healed. We shall march quickly. Past Kenmore Square."

"Ah, I know where you want to go. St. Aloysius Hospital for Lost and Forgotten Children. Most folks just say or know it as St. Aloysius Hospital. You are blessed in spirit. Once we get parallel to Kenmore Square, we shall cross onto the Charles River, and walk up the snow packed ice. None shall follow us. If everyone walked on the ice, it might not hold up," Santa's eyes sparkled in glee, as he was proud of his new idea.

"We shall walk on water!" another soldier hooted.

"So to speak," the elf chastised him a bit.

They marched on. Dozens were healed unknowingly. It was so bitterly cold, they did not feel the energy, nor see the white light against the backdrop of the city lights and white snowbanks. Most were already so invigorated, they did not feel a more youthful energy and appearance. Only the next day would they bask in their new-found youthful appearance and good health. Nagging injuries, annoying infirmities, visible scars, and awkward deformities would be gone. It was The Awakening.

The chorus of voices was rising. The National Guard was around to keep the order, but it was orderly. They were part of the throngs, like the people. The President was on full alert. Unknown to the world, the President was on his way to Boston on Air Force One. He wanted to be in Boston, even though security would be impossible. But the healer would protect him. That he was sure of.

I want my youth. I want my complete health. I am the leader of the free world. The healer must meet with me. He must meet with the President as a sign of peace and cooperation with his world, whether it be another alien world, spiritual world, Atlantis, parallel universe, or heaven itself.

Jackhammer had been silent. A few mumblings and musings kept his listeners tuned in. But then he awoke.

"Breaking News Again. All of the major highways into the city, Interstates 90 and 93 and Route 1 have been blockaded. No more cars or trucks in the city. The mayor has announced the City is closed and in lock down. All subways and commuter rails into the city have been suspended. No traffic is permitted on the Boston streets. Cars are stranded everywhere. There is no place for cars to move. More information. All local streets with ingress into the city are closed off. The National Guard is closing off these streets. There are hundreds of thousands of people in the streets. There is no more room for any more people. But the businesses of this great city are helping. All establishments have been opened up for people to warm up and use the restrooms. The subway system is open to take outbound trains. The stations are open for people to get warm and then head back out, or to use the restrooms. People are handing out cookies and bottles of water."

Jackhammer took a big breath.

"Well, this is Jackhammer! Are you not going to thank me for bringing the story of the healer to all of you? Would the healer not have simply gone back home without my excellent coverage of the Massachusetts Avenue miracles? Yes, stay tuned to me tonight for dramatic coverage. There is a secret I have been keeping, too. Stay tuned to hear!"

"What is the secret! Anna? St. Aloysius Hospital! Of course, what a way to go out for the healer. Although, I suspect people think there will be a mass healing. Where were you on December 27, a day of healing, will be the cry," Sandy looked to the future with one eye, as her other eye kept glued to the video streams.

"Yes, that would be a major scoop, but not a secret, if Savannah finds the healer before he leaves through the Portal. No, though, I want to tell everyone about Savannah," Jackhammer shook, while he stared back at Sandy.

Sandy said nothing but nodded.

"Look, the city lights just went out!!" Sandy then shouted.

"Is our power still on?" Jackhammer panicked.

"Yes, our video feeds are still coming in."

"But your smartphone and computer are on battery power!"

Sandy looked perplexed and then fearful. The lights then went out.

Winston saw the city street lights flicker, then dim, then flicker out. Windows were no longer visible, as their internal light waves disappeared into the ether. The candle lights were bright for the people. And then the moon burst through the clouds. The sky cleared. It was not a miracle. It had been the forecast. But it appeared as a miracle. But why did the power go out? The Mayor and Governor knew. They were behind it. They were fully immersed in The Awakening.

All could see with the silvery light of the moon. Candles burned brightly for the needed close-range vision for curbs, and potholes. Smartphones were lighting up the streets. Video streams and audio streams were omnipresent. This was not a blackout from the 1980s. A mini-baby boom was not on the way. Warmth was not an issue for those inside. Warmth was not an issue outside either, as the masses huddled together as one. The people then went silent for a moment. The screams, chants, singing, bellows, laughter, and talking stopped in their tracks. Phones were silent. Hundreds of thousands of people suddenly were silent.

A light breeze blew. It was if it was the breath of God himself. The people shivered not in cold but in acceptance and acknowledgment of the breath of God that touched their souls. This is what they thought and believed. The silence was broken as Jackhammer took the opportunity to spread his word.

"The power and lights are out, for the rest of the world to know. But the people are calm and at peace. The silvery moon alights the streets. The people await the healer. More miracles will soon come. This is The Awakening. In Boston. May this day of healing live forever in our hearts and minds."

Savannah had left Beacon Street. She never met Becca. She crossed Storrow Drive, now closed to all traffic. She walked to the path along the Charles River. She saw a small group head out over the Charles River and head west. They were heading west towards the bridge, past Kenmore Square and across from the hospital. As she went to take her first step on to the ice an arm grabbed her. She turned and hoped for the best.

It was not the healer. But just as well. It was Becca. They embraced warmly.

"I found you! I prayed to St. Anthony that I would find you, and together we would find the healer! Oh, Savannah, you have meant so much to me as my friend, and now, you saved my life! Thank you so much! Forever!"

"Becca, I am so happy for you. Do you know that my soul had left my body? I was attached by a single thread. There is more to life than our conscious minds will ever know. And not that anyone cares, but mathematics can prove most of these miracles, at least the Portal theories, and parallel universes. And science can prove the existence of alien life. I am not sure if the existence of our souls can be proven by science or mathematics, but I saw my soul's existence outside my body. I felt my soul and spirit. It was not a dream or the mind playing games on death. It was me. And I saw the white light. As did you. That is a special energy. And one that I hope to quantify and study. But for now, I am not a scientist. I am a part of The Awakening. Part of this larger force that the healer has brought with him. He whispered in my ear, that he was a King, that I was healed, and that I was to serve the common good. And so, I shall," Savannah left the embrace of Becca.

"He whispered the same into my ears. He mentioned Atlantis. I think he is somehow affiliated with Atlantis. I had a dream about Atlantis, but maybe it was heaven," Becca teared up.

"Becca, your hair! It is so long and lustrous!"

Becca picked up her cap. It had fallen off when she embraced her friend.

"I think Atlantis is not necessarily the place of Plato. It may be in another parallel realm. Whatever the healer believes, that is good. It works! And now let's hope St. Anthony leads us to the healer!"

Becca smiled and agreed.

"Look, with the lights out, the snow on the Charles River is so bright in the moonlight. Look there are people walking on the ice. Are they safe? Were you following them. Omigod! Is it the healer? If so, we must get him to Anna!" Becky screamed.

"I think it may be the healer! St. Anthony is working his miracles again! Let's catch up and join them and see for sure. It looks like all men. They could use a couple of good women!" Savannah laughed.

Savannah's long blonde hair momentarily flopped in the breeze across her forehead and shoulders. Her blue eyes took on a silvery tint in the moonlight, as if her eyes were lit up by a force in another dimension. Becca shivered at the sight. Both Savannah and Becca, now healed, were runners and good athletes. They jogged at a healthy pace to join the men marching on the river. When they caught them, Savannah and Becca saw it was indeed the healer. They secretly thanked St. Anthony.

11.

J ACKHAMMER HUNG UP THE PHONE. He was so thrilled. His sister had found the healer. She told her brother they were near Kenmore Square, but did not tell him they were on the snow-covered ice on the Charles River, under the silvery light of the winter moon. She told her brother what she had learned. The healer had been on his way to St. Aloysius Hospital the night before, until he saved her! And the two men who were known as Santa and the elf were there with the healer, too. She told her brother what she had learned about them, too. Santa and the elf were two veterans, both of whom had lost their legs in combat. They had been behind the boathouse on the Charles River across from the hospital, where, even in the cold, they reminisced about their times on tour, and their lost buddies at war. Never before had they ventured out on their wheelchairs, without assistance, in such cold and wintery conditions. But they felt a calling. They had taken the subway up past Kenmore Square from their soldier's home and wheeled themselves over the bridge over the Charles River, and then down to the boathouse, all in sight of the hospital. They watched the cars travel down Memorial Drive and Storrow Drive.

And then they saw the white light shoot across the sky. Shivers went down their spines. Soon they saw a man walking towards them. They saw a glimmer of white light emanating from his right hand. They trembled even more. Soon he approached them. He put his hand on one of them and whispered in his ear. He repeated the ritual for the other.

"Go and serve the common good."

The man left. They stared at each other. They pondered what had happened. Soon they both realized they had been healed, their legs fully restored. They jumped out of their wheel chairs and yelled and whooped for joy. Afterwards, they were reflective.

"Remember we were talking this morning. That The Awakening was nearing, and that Boston was to be the starting point. That people would return in flocks to the Lord and their God. The white light. It must have been the man. The man that healed us. The healer. Or the light that infused the man with the power to heal. Or the Holy Spirt. He must be a messenger or prophet from God," the former soldier surmised to his friend.

"And we must spread the word," his friend elf spoke.

"Let's put on our holiday costumes, you as an elf, and me as Santa, and spread the word!"

"People will think we are kooks! But let us spread the word."

The two of them had put on their costumes and walked bravely out on the ice covering the Charles River to the east of and near the bridge near the hospital. On the snow-covered ice they inscribed with their feet the giant message-THE AWAKENING.

Jackhammer belted out the story.

"The healer has been found! He is still in Boston, somewhere in the Back Bay near Kenmore Square! And the two crazy guys dressed as Santa and an elf, who were on the ice-covered Charles River on Thursday night, last night, well, they are with the healer! They were American heroes and wounded soldiers. They were the second and third persons to be healed by the healer. After they were healed, they put on their costumes from a holiday party a few nights ago. They wanted to spread the message. I can now confirm what I speculated before. They inscribed on the snow-covered Charles River the message-THE AWAKENING. But the inscription has been recently wind swept away in the last few hours. All but the big A."

Jackhammer was breathing heavily, reviewing his life for all his misdeeds, and hoping for forgiveness. *There really is an afterlife, a God, a force. Serve others. Serve the common good.*

"And now my secret! I started this story, well, I continued the story after I had heard from John the Baptist, who I know as John from the South End. But this all started last night. My sister, Savannah, was the first person healed by the healer. She was struck by a car on Storrow Drive while running. She was near death. She saw her soul attached to her body by a single thread. And then the white light, and the healer, and she was healed. Her clothes were still blood stained. I believe the white light we saw last night was the first white light, from the healer's first healing. Or it may have been him coming to earth from the Portal right before he healed my sister. Or maybe he was infused by the white light before he healed my sister, yes, that makes sense. Maybe he was infused by the Holy Spirit!" Jackhammer signed off for a break, with no commercials.

Sandy was shaking now, too. She had swept her mind clean and was certain she was cleared for heaven. She could walk through that Portal with her head held high if called upon by the healer. She had spent most of her life helping others. Five times she had participated in Habitat for Humanity. She had volunteered at food banks, and shelters.

She visited soldier's homes. She thought she knew who the elf and Santa were. She had seen them in one of the soldier homes near North Station, where she would bring her famous home baked chocolate chip cookies. She coached inner city kids in lacrosse. And she helped take care of her grandfather, suffering from Alzheimer's. Yes, she was ready. Through the Portal she would go. And she would see her Mom and Dad and younger brother again.

Her brother had died young of a brain tumor. Her Mom and Dad were on a dream vacation to Hawaii. They were a middle-class family. Sandy had earned a partial scholarship to her college for lacrosse. Her parents took that savings and took a trip to Hawaii. They drowned when an unexpected squall overturned their small rented sailboat. She was so grief stricken. They never saw her play. She was an All-American her sophomore year and her team made the NCAA tournament. She was devastated. Then, before her Junior year she developed the same brain tumor her brother had had. She was 20. She was an orphan. Three of her grandparents were gone, and her grandfather was in a nursing home for his Alzheimer's. She had no Aunts and Uncles. She was alone. Her teammates were supportive. But she had to fight this battle. A family friend was a doctor at St. Aloysius Hospital for Lost and Forgotten Children. It was a hospital formed by a foundation of a wealthy billionaire, an orphan himself, who had made billions in the twentieth century in software. The doctor admitted her to the hospital. There was no charge. The endowment for the hospital was safe and secure, managed by the best money management firm in Cambridge.

Sandy recalled her stay on the tenth floor. That was the last stop before heaven. She remembered gazing at the Charles River from the one window looking out that way. The boathouse was teeming with athletes like her. All of her friends on the tenth floor had passed. But she hung on. New kids came. Her last threads of life were seemingly made of tungsten. And then a miracle. A new alternative gene-based therapy. She volunteered. It worked. The therapy soon worked on many others. She was so happy; her test case may have saved others. She missed those who had passed. Now she might see them again, on the other side of this Portal. She did not play lacrosse again but was rewarded a full scholarship for her Junior and Senior years based on need. Her parents were neglectful in one aspect. They only had enough insurance to pay off their debt from her brother's medical expenses, and other debt they had accumulated over the years. So, the scholarship was so welcomed.

"Tell her again to bring the healer to St. Aloysius Hospital for Lost and Forgotten Children! To see Anna!" Sandy blurted out. Jackhammer was resting, and the microphone was off. Otherwise, the crowds would have swarmed the hospital.

"She is going there now."

"Good. You know, I was once a patient there. And I survived the tenth floor, where Anna is. That is their hospice floor, where there is little to no hope. My thread was made of tungsten, and I survived. I want to give back. I want to help bring the healer to Anna and those other kids!" Sandy was openly weeping, both in joy of her memories of recovering, and her concern to help Anna. Forgotten for now, was her upcoming journey through the Portal to heaven, to redemption and reunion with God, and her Lord.

"Savannah said they are heading to St. Aloysius Hospital. Apparently, the healer had intended to go to St. Aloysius Hospital last night, but a certain girl fell to her apparent near death on Storrow Drive! He had a detour! And decided to go today instead. And then he went to Massachusetts

Avenue for a walk, and the miracles came early. Oh, did they come! And thus, his trip to St. Aloysius Hospital was delayed again. But now the healer and his group are going to St. Aloysius Hospital for Lost and Forgotten Children. I hope they can make their way through the massive crowds, and remain unnoticed," Jackhammer said to her, now with his shoulders pulled back.

Sandy and Jackhammer looked at each other. A hurried plan for marriage by the healer had gone by the wayside. A decision that was made on fear of an Apocalypse, or end of the world, possibly. But their eyes shone through to their souls, yes, someday, they would still get married.

"I am not certain, but this may be my last day on earth. Maybe you should join me on my walk through the Portal with the healer. Whether only the good go through the Portal, or if this is the end of days, I don't know. You are a good man, down in your soul. Come with me. Let's head to the boathouse. The Portal must be near there. The masses are in the streets in Boston, not on the river, and not in Cambridge. Come with me to the other side?"

"Sandy, you are now the love of my life. But, I have a duty to the people to keep them informed about The Awakening. Go, I will leave once the healer leaves St. Aloysius Hospital, assuming he gets there. If he is not there soon, I will find you! And if you cross through to the other side, I will find you when I cross, in death, or in ten years, when the healer returns, or the Lord himself comes to see his flock," Jackhammer embraced her for a long moment.

"I will wait until the last moment to leave! I will wait for you on the other side, if that is where I go tonight. I love you in body and soul! Forever!"

They kissed for another long moment. Sandy grabbed her coat and headed for the Back Bay. The outbound subway was still ferrying people out that way, but it was packed, and people were having a difficult time leaving the subway stations for the sidewalks above, as room was scarce.

She decided to walk. She had a plan. The river itself.

Jackhammer watched. He could not bear to see her leave. He found a young intern. The intern was instructed to stay in touch with him by a smartphone with a direct connection to his smartphone and to broadcast his voice on demand. Off he hurried to catch Sandy.

12.

WINSTON PICKED UP HIS SMARTPHONE. He saw his daughter had called him from London. He touched her name on his contact list. She picked up. He recalled he had healed her in London. She was the reason he had gone to London. And then the visions. The cloud formation of a Palace, and a Temple. Soon, he had visions at night, of being a healer and King, in a legendary continent. He knew it was Atlantis. Then the energy. Then the healings. Soon he was with the Queen. A royal ball. There was Becca, the persistent reporter who found him and hooked him up with the Queen. But all had been discreet. There was no Awakening in London.

"Dad, what is going on in Boston. It is in the wee hours of the morning here. But hundreds, even thousands now are in the streets, holding candles, praying silently. The Queen has called me. Becca has called me. They wonder if it is you. Are you the healer in Boston? But this is so beyond what you did in London. There was no mass hysteria, no people in the street begging for salvation. Are you safe? Can you feel the power of this other healer? Is he a prophet? Is he a messenger from God? What is this talk of a Portal? Is he from another universe or part of our universe? Has he reached out to you? Has the Lord reached out to you? Is this the end of days? Or really a beginning? A true Awakening to a new age of mankind? But, is it you?"

Winston could hear his daughter's voice tremble in fear, uncertainty and excitement.

"Elizabeth, I have healed some people in Boston. Quite a few. It has led to this mass outpouring of hope. It indeed has sparked The Awakening. The people are praying for salvation and uniting in peace and love. Speculation is rampant on who I am. I am not certain myself. I feel a powerful presence. It may be the Lord, it may be God, it may be the Universal Force from Atlantis. I am being guided by this invisible force. I feel enormous peace with it. I am following its guidance. I certainly did not arrive today through a Portal. But maybe this invisible force did. The Holy Spirit maybe has come through this Portal. There was a bright white light last night that lit the sky for the tiniest of moments. It flowed through me. I saw it and felt it. It happened right before I healed a young woman who had been nearly fatally stricken by a car while jogging near Storrow Drive. She had a thread of life left. I was able to heal her. With the bolt of white light, I was infused with tremendous energy. Maybe it is the energy of the crystals from Atlantis, which I had always assumed was my source of power for my healing, tapped through the higher spiritual realms. But I am thinking now that it is from a larger or greater being or force. Maybe the crystals draw from this same force. They have talked of The Awakening for some time starting in Boston. That it would be launched by the Holy Spirit. Maybe, I am a messenger, or servant of the Lord for the Holy Spirit. Maybe Atlantis was real, that the Holy Spirit and Universal Force are one. I was King of Atlantis, and now I have a role in The Awakening of mankind in the current space and time. This is palpable. This is momentous. I march on. You should come home. Or if the people are right, maybe I will be leaving tonight back through that Portal where the Holy Spirit or force came from. I love you!"

Winston shed a tear, realizing this might be his last stand. His one final destination to help mankind.

"I love you, too, Dad. I will not tell them it is you. I will come home soon. I hope you stay on earth!" Elizabeth hung up, weeping. But she felt the energy of this magical force from her father's voice, and even his soul. She grabbed a candle. Maybe she could heal now, too.

Winston then texted his wife Mary in Connecticut. "I am in Boston. I am the healer. Keep it hush, for now. I may not be back. I love you! And if I don't make it back home, I will look out for you from afar. Or have an angel look out for you. Maybe buy a lottery ticket tomorrow! Ha! JK. LOL. Love you forever across all dimensions and realms, and heaven, too."

Winston texted his youngest daughter, Anne, too. She was in Vermont skiing. "I love you! I may cross to the other side tonight. Know that I will always be with you!"

"I knew it was you! I want to go with you, too!"

"Stay. You will have an important role. And your first child will be a special child! A future great leader. Yes, stay!"

Winston looked at Savannah.

"Your mathematical formulas are a breakthrough. I think you will have some guidance from now on! The Holy Spirit! The Universal Force! You were saved for a reason. You should start tonight!" Winston had put his arm around her.

She felt the enormous energy she had felt on Storrow Drive the night before. She saw formulas dance in her head. Epiphanies toppled upon her. Her mind was racing as fast as electrons could spark and jump and jostle. Her only constraint was the binary nature of her brain. *I need blockchain brainpower!*

Winston heard her thoughts.

"You will have a visitor tomorrow. He came here for the excitement, and the chance to go to a new world. He is a lifetime science fiction junkie. He wants the Portal. He wants to travel to other dimensions and universes. But he was guided here. I can see that now. He is from Palo Alto. He is a blockchain guru. He will harness it for your math. He wants to discover the Portal in science. The fact that it may indeed exist has launched him into a furious obsession. You may even like him. He actually played lacrosse. I know you played in college."

"May I go back to my university now! Say hello to Anna for me!'

"Sure, go. Becca will stay with us. Maybe I will be your spiritual guide after today, if I go through the Portal!" Winston teared up some more. He liked this Savannah. He knew she was special. He had touched her soul. He saw her entire existence, at least, he thought. A top scientist in Atlantis, with ties to the upper tiers of the spiritual realms. And last night, what Winston was coming to realize, she was touched, through him, by the Holy Spirit, possibly, he imagined, the embodiment of the spirit of his Universal Force from Atlantis.

Savannah headed straight across the river. She stepped on the large A. It had somehow survived. She had always had straight A's, at all levels of education. Now, for mankind, she would help find the path to eternity through math and science. She would prove her religious beliefs. Ones firmly implanted in her forever after her encounter with the healer and the Holy Spirit.

I did not ask him his name. He talked to someone on the phone. It sounded like a father talking to his daughter. And then he was texting someone, or more than one person, with a tear in his eye.

Maybe he is earthly, and was infused with the Holy Spirit, or his Atlantean Universal Force, to heal. I need to talk to him.

Savannah then decided to return, but before she did, she had something to do. Becca saw she had stopped. Becca hurried over to her.

"Ah, I see!"

Together the two young women carved again the words The Awakening on the snow-covered ice. They then jogged back to catch up with Winston.

Winston was alone now. He had asked the six soldiers, including Santa and the elf, to depart. He noticed people saw his group on the ice, and some had sojourned onto the glistening snow pack. He feared they would follow him and more would follow. The soldiers shook his hand. He imbued them with energy to be leaders. They puffed their chests, bellowed, and ran in military formation to clear the river of people. Their newfound limbs were brimming with life. They stopped at one point and turned to face Winston. They stood at attention and saluted him. They turned back in unison and ushered people off of the ice. The elf looked back one last time, and then left.

Savannah caught up to Winston. Becca did as well. Each woman grabbed one of his arms. They all held each other in balance on the snow-covered ice. They were now past Kenmore Square and not far from the hospital. Savannah thought about calling Anna but held off. Who knows what type of tempest might be created if the staff and patients knew the healer was coming. No, the plan would be to go directly to the tenth floor to see Anna. Jackhammer and Sandy had asked Savannah and Becca to find and usher the healer to the hospital. Now, it was time to finish the mission.

Sandy had told Jackhammer her story. He had not known. Jackhammer had then told Savannah. She did not know Sandy in person, but now felt a tight bond with her. She even broke down for a moment.

Winston noticed she was silently sobbing.

"Sandy, the producer on the show with my brother, Jackhammer, was on that tenth floor. She really wants us to make it there."

"That is the plan, and has been since last night, as I told you. We will get there," the healer assured her.

Becca and Savannah held each of his arms very tightly. Winston gazed at the silvery moon. He saw a break in the crowd along the snow-packed path next to the river. The three of them soon exited the river. The bank had some steepness. The two women, wearing good winter boots, climbed the bank first, and then pulled up Winston. They sat on a bench, that was cleared of snow, for a respite.

"We don't know your name, or who you are," Becca softly said, her arms folded across her chest for warmth.

Savannah took a deep breath.

"You were talking to someone. I think it was likely your daughter. You were texting, too, with a tear in your eye, and then a loving smile. So, you are of this world! You did not come through the Portal, did you?" She exclaimed, but with respect and admiration.

"Becca and Savannah, I healed you both. Savannah, as I have said, you shall achieve greatness in mathematics and science. And maybe understanding of the Portal! Becca, there is a mission for you, as well. You will receive guidance later this weekend."

The two young women wanted more answers. But Winston was silent. He was lost in deep thought. His eyes looked like they were rolling back into his head.

Savannah panicked. She put her two palms on his face and held it firmly.

Winston saw her eyes and returned from his higher state of consciousness.

"Savannah, I believe I have reacquired the powers I had in Atlantis, to freely roam in the spiritual realms. I may soon leave this earth and disassociate with my earthly body. And there is a Portal. I can see it clearly now. I think the Holy Spirit is among us. It is infused into our souls and beings. It was sent by the Lord. It came through the Portal."

Winston then put his palms on her face and held her firmly.

"I firmly believe I once lived in the legendary continent of Atlantis. I was its final King, when it perished into the sea. But its people, those that were of good spirit, had access to the spiritual realms. Some could ascend to see God, what they called the Universal Force. And last night God, or the Universal Force, has sent the Holy Spirit to us through the Portal. The white light was from the Portal. It is time to start The Awakening. Our souls shall be infused with the Holy Spirit and hear the words of the Lord and the Universal Force."

Winston let go of her face.

"I will continue to heal people tonight, including our Anna. But I may leave the earth, as I said, and follow the Holy Spirit back through the Portal. If I live, I likely will revert to my humanly self, and not have healing powers. I once had these powers when I visited my daughter in London in the fall. I healed many. I even met with the Queen. A reporter tried to find me. She eventually did but ultimately did not report the story on my healings. Her name was Becca, too!"

The two women did not know what to say. Becca now knew who Becca was. And her dream was looking more like Atlantis after all.

"On earth, I am Winston Chamberlain. I live in Connect-icut. I have a wife and two adult daughters. I will miss them if I move on. That is my story. It is time to complete our journey!"

With that Winston took the hands of the two women and headed back into the heavy crowds. They now were near St Aloysius Hospital.

"Shall we?"

"Yes!" the two young women shouted.

"And may I join you?" Another young woman asked.

"I can see things clearly now. You are Sandy, from the radio station. You are a good soul. You were saved here once! Of course, you are welcome. And, oh, it is you! The famous and great Jackhammer! Believe it or not, I have lis-tened to you for years. Come join us, too."

Winston seemed to relax.

"One more, sir!"

"Winston turned.

"AH, yes, John the Baptist! Well, you are not him. But, yes, join us."

Jackhammer smiled at John the Baptist.

"A face to a name! Hello, long time caller John from the South End!"

And through the door six of them went to the lobby of St. Aloysius Hospital for Lost and Forgotten Children.

13.

W INSTON LOOKED AT SANDY. They were on the first floor in the reception area of the hospital.

"Come with me, Sandy. You know this place well. Jackhammer, stay here. I know you are hooked up to the radio station to tell all to the world. Sandy will report to you. Savannah and Becca, go to the lower floors, starting on nine and eight, and tell the kids to be patient, stay in their rooms, and not go on social media or to otherwise call anyone. I know none of these kids have family. Smile and tell them how you were healed. Happy thoughts all around."

Winston walked to the receptionist. She was an elder woman. She was feverish in anticipation. She overheard the conversation. It did not take her long to realize who was before her. It was the healer. She cut off all the access lines to the rooms. There were seldom any calls, but if any came in now, they would be blocked. The silent alarm button stayed untouched. She put some tape over it, so she would not accidently set it off. The two security guards on the ground floor, not armed, had left to go to Kenmore Square. Kenmore Square had become the focus of the crowds, as rumors honed in on the location of the Portal as near or in Kenmore Square. Both had chronic ailments and did not want to miss out on any healing. She acquiesced. Some paramedics had called and volunteered to bring Anna and one more child to Kenmore Square. She declined, saying the cold air would kill them on the spot. She told them they were angels for asking. One said he thought the healer was responsible for saving a victim on Storrow Drive the night before. She had heard the story. And then heard Jackhammer's version. The paramedic must have been one the few in the city not to hear Jackhammer tell the world how his sister was the first one healed by the healer.

The elder woman noticed now that Jackhammer was in her midst. She adored him and his show. She gasped. And it dawned on her that the tall svelte blonde must be his sister, all the better from her brush with death, and then the angelic or Holy power of the healer. She trembled as she watched them.

Winston walked behind the receptionist's oak desk and grabbed both of her hands. He whispered into her ear. He waved his right hand over her head and shoulders. White light lit up the room. Boundless white light burst from Winston. The elder woman fainted in joy and exhaustion. Her liver disease and other ailments from a former life of alcoholism and drug addiction, were gone forever. She had beaten both, but her body was a skeleton and a broken-down version of her once beautiful self. Becca marveled and then almost fell to the floor when she noticed the elder woman was no longer elder. She was now a brilliantly beautiful thirty something year old. Savannah gasped, too. The woman was a once well-known, but now long forgotten, movie star from Boston who had hit the big screen pay-dirt in a big way, only to wither it away in alcoholism, and addiction. No longer. A second chance. The world would receiver her in open arms, Savannah thought.

Winston summoned John from the South End.

"John, tonight you shall indeed play the role of your new namesake. Come with Sandy and me. Jackhammer, have the receptionist take notes from Sandy, when she awakes. You will have so much to report. Give Sandy a warm hug, too."

"Ok," Jackhammer was taken aback. But he gave Sandy the warmest of embraces.

He wanted to ask the healer to marry Sandy and him but hesitated and then blinked. It was too late. Sandy saw the hesitation. She looked away though. Much to the concern of Jackhammer.

Savannah and Becca split up. Savannah started on the eighth floor. Becca on the ninth. Each floor represented a greater degree of seriousness of the afflictions for the children. Sometimes a child would climb the ladder, as the kids called it, progressing to darker stages of their illnesses. But others went down the slide, as the kids called it, as they progressed to the bright side. When a child slid all the way down the slide, to the open air of the outside world, bells would ring and all the kids would cheer. When a child passed, the lights would dim. All the kids would pray for their lost friend and soul. Down deep, many believed in a happy other side, one where family and departed friends, and angels and even God waited for them.

Now the kids had followed the story of the healer. They were all connected on one social network that only they could post on, and only they could share, and like, and chat and email and text. They called it the St. Aloysius Kids Portal or SAKPORT for short. Today it had been lit up. And Anna was the Queen of the Portal. She had told the kids about the jogger that was saved. About the wheelchairs by the boathouse. The inscription in the snow-covered Charles River. All day the kids listened to Jackhammer. The Massachusetts Avenue miracles. The Quincy market healings. The woman's son. Then the name to the Storrow Drive jogger and saved one. It was Jackhammer's only sister! More stories. Santa and the elf. They giggled over that one. The description of the Portal. They had always called their network the Portal, long before the healer had come through the Portal. And there was John the Baptist. The kids talked of being healed, then talked of being saved, or finding salvation, or going through a real-life Portal to the other side without waiting for a painful death to their earthly bodies. Excitement was rampant. Kids knocking on death's door simply stopped knocking. They were not going to miss today. No way.

There were two nurse night shifts, each with two nurses per floor. The first was 6 p.m. to midnight, the second from midnight to 7 a.m. Doctors, specialists, day shift nurses, PAs and NPs traversed the floor during the working hours. It was now 7 p.m. The doctors, specialists, PAs and NPs had left, as had the daytime nurses. The first shift nighttime nurses were all glued to their smart devices, streaming videos of Kenmore Square, but with Jackhammer's station on in the background for audio.

Becca approached the head nurse on the ninth floor. Winston, who now seemed to have omniscience, had told her of the SAKPORT.

"The healer is here! He is starting with Anna on the tenth floor. The kids are all going to know. You know, the SAKPORT," Becca held her index to her lips. Becca was still wearing her winter cap.

The nurse looked up, ignoring her. Then, she snapped to attention.

"Omigod! He is here. The kids have been praying and singing all day for him to come. They seemed so sure he would come. And he is here! Oh! Oh!" the nurse collapsed in her chair weeping in joy and relief.

Becca removed her coat and cap and rested it on an empty chair next to the nurses' desk. Her hair was lustrous still, full of magical energy. Her skin was radiant. She was so beautiful now.

Becca raised the nurse to her feet.

"I need you now. You will be healed, too. But I need you to control these kids. Keep them off any network other than the SAKPORT. Tell the kids to tell the other kids on other floors to stay on their floors. Be patient. Their time will come. They shall be healed. Hoorah! Hooray! Alleluia! Hosanna in the Highest! Salvation! Lord have mercy on us! The doorway to heaven is open, if only for such a brief moment. The Awakening has begun. And in our great city of Boston!"

Becca was now shaking, too. She was suddenly an orator!

Two sickly kids had peeked out behind the doorways of their rooms. The other nurse headed to scurry them back to their beds. But it was too late. The kids screamed at the top of their weak lungs. Soon other kids were out of their beds. Bedlam was rampant. The kids flocked to Becca. They surrounded her and serenaded her. They hugged and kissed her. They figured her as an assistant angel. They started singing. But Becca noticed they had not accessed the SAKPORT, not yet.

Becca raised her hands in the air. The kids were dutifully silent. They were the ninth-floor kids. They were not knocking on death's door like the tenth-floor kids. But many would have to climb the ladder to the tenth floor, if later day remedies and clinical trials failed. They were the clinical trial kids. There was hope, but traditional medical treatments did not work for them. Most were cancer patients, but other afflictions were present, too.

Becca told the kids that the healer was indeed in the building. That the healer was infused with the powers of the Holy Spirit, or to him, possibly, the Universal Force, that he was indeed a special being. That he was the former King of the legendary continent of Atlantis, whether on earth or a parallel world. That there is a Portal. That the healer may leave tonight through the Portal. That the Holy Spirit came through the Portal to the healer last night and was still here. That the Lord was waiting on the other side of the Portal. That some of them may go to the Portal to-night, but she did not know. She suspected two or three of her group would go through the Portal tonight. One, likely, the healer. But who else. She and Savannah were both to have died. Maybe their role was to help heal these kids, and then meet their destiny- the Portal. And then there was Sandy. She was here once. Was she returning to finally re-unite with her family on the other side? Part of her wanted to see the other side. It did not seem so fearful now. And that there were some magical in between realms, like a spir-itually advanced and technologically advanced place like At-lantis. *But, Atlantis had crashed into the sea. What of the Atlantean crystals? Were the healings the result of the crystals? Ex-plainable by science and math! Who cares. It is all so boundless and believable now.*

The kids seemed to hear her every thought as well as her every word. The kids should have been wiped out and thor-oughly exhausted from their day of dreaming and wishing and hoping and praying. But the energy level spiked. Becca felt it. The kids seemed to draw more energy from her hair. She gave each kid a locket. They roared.

A chant arose.

"We are the kids! We are the kids! We are the kids of At-lantis! We are the kids of the Portal! We are the kids of the Holy Spirit! We are the kids of The Awakening! The first kids to be awakened!"

They held hands and went around and around in circles and then throughout the floor, like a line dance at a wedding.

And it was all recorded on the SAKPORT!

Savannah was on the eighth floor. The kids were not terminal, nor on experimental drugs. Most expected to go down the slide, although historically, it was a 50-50 proposition. Nevertheless, they had more energy. Savannah had informed both nurses. No kids had eavesdropped. But the streaming video of the ninth floor had gone viral! All the floors three to seven were hysterical but controlled. Her kids were beaming with excitement, but controlled, waiting for her guidance. A new message then was sent by Savannah on one of the kid's smartphones to Anna. Have the kids stay on their floors! Anna successfully sent the message across to all the kids on the other floors. The ninth-floor nurse notified the nurses on the other floors, too. Anna's kids, the kids on the tenth floor, had fallen asleep. The day was too much. Anna secretly worried the energy spent on hope, was their last swing at death. But the healer was coming.

The lower floors rocked and gyrated but stayed on their floors. Sandy passed the information on to Jackhammer. He said he would wait until the kids on the tenth floor were healed before he announced the upcoming healings to the world. Sandy said why not wait until all the kids in the hospital were healed. Jackhammer was not sure.

14.

ECCA AND SAVANNAH LEFT THEIR FLOORS to join the healer, John the Baptist and Sandy on the tenth floor. The nurses on each floor below the tenth floor corralled their kids and had them caroling vociferously. There seemed to be no shortage of energy and enthusiasm. Today was the day. The mantra repeated relentlessly. Sandy was by herself, on a couch near the window. She was gazing at the Charles River, and the white snow, so bright from the silvery moonlight. Memories. Vivid memories cascaded through her mind. She had been saved by medicine and science. But every other kid on her floor had not lived. She carried that with her, a heavy weight around her neck.

She looked down now. To her surprise, she saw the heavy weight, held by heavy chains, all pulling her down. She had never seen it before. She looked back. There was Anna. Anna saw the chains and weight, too. She made a motion of lifting the chains over her neck and tossing the weight aside. Sandy beamed. She followed her directions, and soon removed the chains and weight. For a moment, she felt so light. She thought she was flying around the tenth floor, like she did in her dreams, often at night. Was her spirit free at night? Was it free now? Had she just died? Oh?

She touched and pinched herself. She was still alive, still corporeal. She smiled broadly at Anna. Your turn.

The healer went to the two nurses, first. Each one he healed. Both were otherwise healthy, but now noticeably a lot more youthful. They tossed back their now lustrous hair, and hugged Winston with joy.

"It is time. Wake the kids. Prepare them. Let them feel the energy seeping up from the bottom floors. The ladder now brings up energy and healing power and auras. The ladder is no longer a death sentence. It's an upside-down world for now. But the slides are still wonderful. All the kids will go down the slides today. All shall be free. All shall be healed. So it shall be said, so it shall be done."

Winston raised his hands high into the air, as if praying to his deity, his God, his Lord, his Universal Force. Sandy dropped to her knees and prayed. Savannah and Becca joined her. John the Baptist, not knowing what to do, grabbed a bottle of water. He baptized the three women. Anna rushed over. She asked to be baptized.

Winston looked on. The three young women and one young girl felt holy and blessed, and part of the new kingdom created by The Awakening. They were the first to be blessed and baptized, they thought. The first Apostles, they surmised.

Anna passed out. Her energy had dissipated. She was near death. Winston looked at the tiny thread holding onto her soul. It was similar to the one that kept Savannah barely alive. Savannah, Sandy and Becca, now baptized, saw the thread, too. John did not. Winston pondered the baptisms. Yes, they were baptized. New angels. Must they now return through the Portal with me? I hope they can stay back here on earth. But not Sandy.

The three young women placed their hands upon Anna. They willed the white light to come. It did not come. They desperately stared back at Winston. Winston stared back at the hallway. The nurses had brought a young Indian boy, also near death to be healed. He had two threads holding him to earth. Winston had to act quickly to save both of them. He saw Anna's thread strengthen with the bonding by his three angels, as he thought of them now. He walked over to the Indian boy. The boy shuddered and collapsed. But the healer caught him and healed him with white light filling the room. The boy jumped from his arms and bounced off the floor in fluid motion and jumped to his feet and then up in the air, his fists pumping wildly.

He cheered and then screamed so loudly, that a roar from the lower floors soon reverberated back up through the stairways to the tenth floor. The building that housed the hospital soon appeared to be alive. It was swaying with all the emotion and energy.

Winston grabbed the Indian boy's hand. Together they walked over to see Anna. The six hands of his three angels firmly held Anna on earth. Winston whispered into her ear, and then into the ear of the Indian boy. He placed his hand on her heart. Anna arose. Her life cord now sturdy and strong. She was healed. Her Teddy Bear smiled. All saw the white light again. The two nurses lost another ten years off their age. From sixties to forties since the healer arrived. Would they hit the thirties? They giggled momentarily, but then there was business to be done. There were ten kids on the floor. Eight to go. Eight more apostles one of them thought. Winston said no. Angels, perhaps. Anna handed her Teddy Bear to Sandy. She teared up.

The roar from the floors below was palpable. White light was streaming out of the tenth-floor window. It was noticed by some people on the street. One knew what the tenth floor was. He shouted out as loud as he could that miracles were happening at St. Aloysius Hospital. The healer was still on earth. He had not left through the Portal just yet. The crowd stirred and then rocked. It was so large, that no one could run or move very far. The streaming white light stopped. The crowd dismissed the man's antics. Similar rejoicing and shouts had occurred throughout the evening. Most were waiting for the official word from Jackhammer. He was rumored to be with the healer and John the Baptist. And his sister, Savannah, had now been canonized by the crowd, and the world media as a saint. St. Savannah she was.

The crowd roared again. Smartphones were buzzing. The Cardinal of the Catholic Church announced officially that The Awakening had indeed begun in Boston. The healer was real. That he was sent by God to start The Awakening. That he healed through and with the power of the Holy Spirit. That a Portal was real and was a pathway to and from heaven. The Pope officially canonized St. Savannah as the first to healed in The Awakening. The crowd roared her name. A real live saint in their midst.

But the crowd then in unison knelt and prayed. The Awakening had begun. Some wailed, others cried, others smiled with joy. Energy was building. Hundreds of thousands were now in Boston. The energy surrounded them and started to emanate from them as well. Some were concerned that they would simply float away to some other dimension, or realm. Some hoped they were on their way to heaven. Some feared the archfiend would snatch them away at the last minute and take them to Hades or hell. No one knew for sure. Those with faith and hope, just believed. Others enjoyed the world's biggest outdoor party. Some met what they were sure were their soulmates, whether for this life or life in the new realms.

Sandy took Winston's hand. She was trembling again. Sandy lead him to Room 1008. Anna was in Room 1010, the darkest of rooms, where the sickest of the girls were placed. It was thought of by the kids, as the real Portal to the other side. No one had ever survived Room 1010. Kids left through that Portal to parts unknown. There was never a white light. The kids hoped it was to the other side where departed relatives and angels and cherubs awaited. But now Anna was alive and well. Jumping two feet in the air. Showing her remarkable gymnastic ability, so long restrained, and hidden. The Indian boy was in Room 1009. It was also a Portal to the other side. No kid had ever survived Room 1009.

Anna texted in the SAKPORT that the kids in Rooms 1010 and 1009 were healed. The rooms were bright white now. Again, the building shook. The loudness was deafening. The crowd outside looked up. They could hear the cheers inside. A collective shiver went through all of them as if they were one unified being. The shiver traveled like electricity through an electric power line all the way to Kenmore Square and beyond. It was a wave that went all the way down Commonwealth Avenue, Beacon Street, deep into the financial district and out to the Seaport District. Where ever people were connected through touch the shiver was felt.

Kids on the third floor had been fully healed. Their ailments were such that the white light and energy generated by all the joyous and jacked and pumped kids that dissipated through the building was enough to heal them. Collectively, they roared, and stormed up to the fourth floor.

Jackhammer stormed up the stairway. He saw the kids on three were healed. He was so excited he forsake his promise to hold off announcing to the world the healer's location and healing actions at the hospital until the tenth-floor kids were healed. He instantly announced to the world that the kids on the third floor of St. Aloysius Hospital had been healed by the healer. That the kids were on their way to the fourth floor, joyously singing, Alleluia, Hosanna in the Highest.

The shiver of the crowd turned into a tremor. The bodies of all the people seemed to be coming together as one being. Glimpses of white light were popping up all around.

A buzzing noise with a powerful white headlight approached. It hovered and headed up Commonwealth Avenue towards Kenmore Square. Many fainted. They thought it was God himself. Others were certain this was a conspiracy and a set up. Others surmised that the aliens were now attacking and would kill them all. Panic started to infiltrate the crowds. Any type of panic could turn into an all-out fleeing of the crowd. Thousands would be trampled and hurt or killed.

It's a helicopter, many shouted. The crowd calmed. The shivers and tremors momentarily gone. The aliens were not attacking yet. God was not coming yet to take them to heaven. It was a news reporter to be sure.

But others saw the Presidential Seal. It was the President of the United States. He was here to see the healer. He could not wait for the healer to come see him. He had taken a helicopter from the White House to Joint Base Andrews, and then Air Force One to Hanscom AFB. And now he was flying in on a helicopter. The helicopter had flown out around Boston to sea, waiting for information on where the healer was. On hearing the healer was at St. Aloysius, it veered over Boston and up Commonwealth Avenue. The prophet, the leader of the alien world, the messenger, the angel, the King of Atlantis. It did not matter. The leader of the free world had to meet him. It was right and just and proper. Plus, he wanted his youth back. He wanted more years of power and success. All the wrong reasons to see an angel.

A police escort was coming from Commonwealth Avenue the other way. It was the Cardinal. He was going to meet the healer as well, as official spokesman of the Catholic Church. Other religious leaders of the world, of all denominations, had flown to Logan Airport. They requested that the U.S. government give them helicopter transportation to see the healer. A world convention would be had. The President agreed. But he was to be the chairman of the meeting. The helicopters were lined up. As word of the location of the healer was spread, the helicopters prepared to leave. Soon a convoy would be heading down Commonwealth Avenue. The crowds would not see a Presidential seal. Fear might strike. Panic might strike. Winston felt the pressure of the crowd. He could see alternate paths to the night. As if he were a quantum physicist, he could see all the possible outcomes. He knew time was of the essence. He had to avert panic and fear.

But Sandy looked deep into his eyes as she stood by the doorway to Room 1008. Winston saw her lying in that bed years ago. Waiting to die. Waiting to see her parents. But then she had been called in to try a new experimental treatment. It had worked. Winston saw the joy in her eyes from that magical day when she went down the slide. Back to her life. Back to college. But she had been the last survivor from Room 1008. Winston walked over to her. She pulled Winston to the bedside of the little nine year African-American girl, a life-long foster child, and now a warden of St. Aloysius Hospital in Room 1008. She once had blinding speed, before she was ill. Even Olympic potential speed. And she could jump forever. She had dreamt over and over while she lay in her bed, of winning the 100-meter hurdle Gold medal for the United States, in the 2032 Olympics, and the triple jump as well. She had envisioned running around the four-hundred-meter track with the American flag wrapped around her shoulders, with two Jamaican girls, the Silver and Bronze medalists, running at her side, to the giant and adoring roar of the crowd. But the dream was now black and white and blurry. She was not sure it was her face anymore that she saw. And the Jamaican girls seemed to laugh at her. They wore the medals, Gold and Silver. She wore no medal. Her life and dreams were draining away. Her pain was muffled by the drugs.

"Save her!" Sandy softly said, as she grabbed the little girl's hand from under the sheet.

Winston kissed Sandy on the cheek.

"You are a good soul. You shall be rewarded in the next realm. In Heaven. This is your last moment on earth. You shall now go through the Portal. This is where you once were destined to go, through the Portal. Now, you shall go. It shall be peaceful. You shall see the Lord. I will see you soon, I am sure," Winston felt a tear stream down his cheek.

Winston leaned over and put his hand on the young girl's forehead. He whispered into her ear. White light enveloped her body. Her soul rejoiced. Before she awoke, there she was leaning across the finish line, just ahead of the two Jamaican hurdlers. A Gold medal was hers. Her eyes opened in jubilation. She saw the healer. She slapped him five for her recent victory and jumped out of her bed. She sprinted to the hallway to join Anna and the Indian boy. They held hands, and played ring around the rosy, laughing loudly and cheerfully.

Winston saw Sandy smile. He saw the Portal coming to them. It opened. White light streamed out of the Portal. Across the Portal, Sandy saw the spirits of her father and mother and brother. She kissed Winston on the cheek.

"Thank you for saving this little girl. I have been haunted that I was the only one ever saved from this room. Now, she is saved. Sandy collapsed. Winston saw her life thread snap, as her soul traversed through the Portal. Winston placed her body in the bed in Room 1008. He covered her face with sheets. He knew how happy she was. But he knew how sad Jackhammer would be. And then Winston saw the body was gone. The Teddy Bear, too. Meanwhile, Savannah, taking over for Sandy on informing Jackhammer, had called her brother to tell him the news of Anna, and the Indian boy in Rooms 1009, and then the girl in Room 1008, when she saw her jumping around with Anna and the Indian boy.

"People of the world. The healer is at work. As I told you moments before, the kids on floor three have been healed of their wounds, all victims of accidents and fires, none life threatening. The white light has healed them. And now, three children from the tenth floor, including Anna, who is the leader of the kids in the hospital, have been healed. Only a few kids have ever been healed on that floor. And Anna and an Indian boy, are the first ever to survive from Rooms 1010 and 1009. Another girl has survived Room 1008 tonight with Sandy, yes, Sandy from the radio station, my producer, at her side. Sandy once was in Room 1008 and survived! They are the only survivors of Room 1008. Miracles at St. Aloysius Hospital continue. White light is everywhere in the hospital. I think the Portal has moved here. And the President of the United States is on his way here, as are world religious leaders, and the Cardinal. Rejoice! Alleluia!"

Outside the crowds roared in unison at the news of the healings. Many knew of the tenth floor. Tears of joy filled many of their eyes. Energy was rampantly flowing through the crowd.

Winston went to Room 1007. A young boy, an immigrant from Bolivia, whose parents had left him with his Grandmother, when they returned to Bolivia, was barely awake. He did not have much cognitive ability left, afflicted with a ravaging disease to his brain. Anna walked in with Winston.

"His name is Jorge'. He was so funny. But then he could not speak, then he could not hear. He can barely see. But, look, he always smiles. He is such a nice boy. His Grandmother used to take care of him. But she died three months ago. He is a lost boy, for sure, like the rest of us. All forgotten. Except by the nice doctors and nurses here. We don't have many visitors, except the couple weeks before Christmas," Anna's eyes welled up.

"Can you still heal?"

"Of course, I can. You can help!"

Winston placed her hands on the boy's folded hands that lay over his stomach. It was as if he was already dead. He whispered into the little boy's ear. He placed his right hand on top of Anna's hands. White light filled the room.

The little boy's eyes lit up. He laughed as loud as he could. His laughter was so loud, that the Indian boy and the Olympian girl rushed in. It also woke up the teenage girl in Room 1006.

Winston swiftly walked to Room 1006. The nurse had the radio on. He heard Jackhammer announce to the world that the child in Room 1007 was healed. An informational highway had been formed from Savannah to Jackhammer. He could hear a thunderous roar outside. The nurse had opened the windows. The healing and white light had raised the room temperature on the floor. Winston felt a cool rush of air from the window flow across his forehead. The mild perspiration was washed away. In the distance he heard a chopper.

Room 1006 housed a teenage girl. She was severely deformed from a horrendous fire in a Boston suburb. Her entire family had perished. She had lived, as she had chased her new puppy out the back door. The puppy died of smoke inhalation. She was 90% burned, and her shoulder and face had been crushed by a falling beam. She had not been found until the next morning. She had crawled under a trash bin in the back yard. With no insurance, and no family, she was admitted to St. Aloysius Hospital for Lost and Forgotten Children. She started on the seventh floor. But her depression and despondence had sapped her strength and the will to live. Up the ladder she went. Right to Room 1006. Rooms 1001 to 1007 carried no special meaning. They were all considered equal. Only Rooms 1008 to 1010 were for kids not expected to live more than a few days, or sometimes hours. Anna had blown away that postulation. The Indian boy was on his fourteenth hour. A lucky hour forever to him now. The Olympic hurdler was on her fourth day. She had been in Room 1001. But they moved her, as her thread of life was limp and tiny.

The teenage girl was giggling. The infectious laugh of the Bolivian boy in Room 1007 had infected her with laughter. She had not laughed since the Bolivian boy had gone silent. Her eyes were wide with anticipation. She leaned up to Winston and put her arms around him. She squeezed him so hard. She had closed her eyes, and then opened them. The other four kids were in her doorway. They were healed. They were healthy. They looked so marvelous. They were beaming. They were electrified with white light. And broad smiles crossed their cherub faces. Then the booming laughter of the Bolivian boy. The contagious laughter soon boomed from the other three kids. Another man laughed with a guttural roar. It was John. She had listened to the radio in the morning, filling her heart with hope. But she had fainted in exhaustion. She had slept through all of the commotion on her tenth floor, until that memorable and loving laugh had belted out and filled her ears.

Winston picked her up. Although a teenager, she was only ninety pounds. He whispered into her ear. White light enveloped her. Her deformities fleeted away. Her burn marks melted into soft beautiful skin that radiated. The Bolivian boy fell to his knees in love. He was twelve, but old enough for a fourteen-year old girlfriend, he thought.

Savannah saw Anna hold the hand of the Indian boy. Savannah looked at John the Baptist for a moment. No, she thought with a laugh. John the Baptist had seen the glimpse. He was widowed. For a second, he thought he was in the game. But the glance was short lived. He turned, though, and there was one of the now younger nurses, watching him. She smiled. He knew he had a new friend, and maybe more. The Olympian girl smiled, too. She knew who was in Room 1005. The next room. A boy that somehow had found his way into her Olympic dreams. He was the announcer for the track and field events for the network broadcasting the Olympics. She could always hear him doing the play by play for football games in his loud voice, watching Patriots games, with the sound off. He was her age. He was African American, too. He had been homeless since he was ten. He was in a car accident, causing him to lose use of his legs, and his right arm. He was not at St. Aloysius for long. Just since mid-December. He had developed a horrific blood infection a few days ago. And was certain to pass soon. He was scheduled to move to her room after she passed. Together they would either go to the Olympics or go to the other side.

She marched into the Room 1005 with Winston. She lay next to him. He was still asleep, heavily medicated. She whispered into his ear, and then laughed when she looked at Winston.

"I remember what you said to me, you know!" She teased.

"Thank you, I shall heal him now, right away!"

Winston placed his hands on the boy's shoulder and his forehead. White light filled his body. The infection evaporated away. His limbs rejuvenated. He bolted upright. He saw Winston, and just started to cry. Then he saw an Olympian next to him.

"I have seen you in my dreams, ever since my infection. You win the Gold medal! I am an announcer. Now, you are here next to me! Am I in heaven now?"

"No, I was in Room 1008. You were to take my place, but I survived. And now you have, too. The healer has healed us. Four more to go! Shall we be friends?" She blushed.

"So, it shall be said, so it shall be done!"

"I wonder where you heard those words!"

All six kids, Savannah, Becca, the two nurses, and John the Baptist hustled to Room 1004. There was a young eight-year old. She had been a daughter of an affluent Investment Money Manager. Her father had died. Her mother then spent all the money, drifting into a life of decadence and drugs. Her mother had finally overdosed. She became a ward of the state. She was stricken with an illness that none could diagnose. She was dying. Only a week left. Her beautiful sky-blue eyes were all that was left of her once adorable confident self. Her shiny blonde hair was matted and gray. Her skin hung from her bones.

Winston walked next to her bed. As he did, a young boy from Room 1003 peered into the room. He was on his last few days. Well past all the treatments for his illness. His body was shot, fallen apart. But his mind was sharp. He had invented an App that had taken off. His foster parents stole it from him once he was sick. He didn't care now. He was homeless and lost and forgotten. But one thing had kept him alive a little longer. He had seen the blue eyes of this little dying girl when she was wheeled in the day after he was admitted. He was mesmerized and in love, he told him-self. He had planned not to die, until just after she did. He was going to chase her on the other side, and frolic in heav-en or wherever they ended up. He dreamed of going to an-other planet in another galaxy with her. He would marry her in that foreign world!

The little girl felt the energy of the other kids. She opened her eyes. Winston saw the little boy. He called him over. Winston pulled the boy's face next to the little girl so that their ears were together. The little boy blushed. Then the little girl blushed. They both giggled. Winston whis-pered into their ears. He could hear the other six kids whis-pering with him with soft breaths. Soon white light enveloped both kids. They smiled effusively. The little boy blurted out that he loved her! She joyously hugged him. Somehow, she knew he was a genius. Winston saw the medal of St. Jude on a necklace around her neck. The little girl saw him look at it, and she smiled back at Winston, touching the medal and mouthing thank you to St. Jude, as a tear trickled down from her eye.

"We shall form an App company together!" the little boy shouted to her.

Well, the kids in Rooms 1001 and 1002, a brother and a sister, and twins, both inflicted with the same terminal rare untreatable cancer, both from West Virginia, and long abandoned by their parents, were lost and forgotten, except they had each other. They had managed to walk the walk. They were in the room. They cheered. Winston picked the twins up, both nine years old. He whispered into their ears. With the white light now abundantly filling the room, he put his forehead one by one against each of their foreheads. They were healed. Spontaneously, Savannah called her brother to report the healings. And the kids, all ten of them ran down the slide to the ninth floor.

Savannah and Becca followed the kids.

St. John the Baptist was with the nurses. They went down to the ninth floor, too.

Savannah had dropped her phone.

Jackhammer had announced to the world that the entire tenth floor had been healed. Winston heard the crowd roar even louder. He picked up Savannah's phone and called Jackhammer.

"Come up to the tenth floor, now if you could." That was all he could say.

He led Jackhammer to the door of Room 1008. Jackhammer had seen the somber look in the healer's eyes. When he saw Room 1008, he buckled. He knew what Room 1008 signified. Sandy had told him on the way over. She had even talked of going through the Portal from that room. He knew, even before he entered the room. He broke down in tears and wept. However, briefly, the power of the day had driven him wildly in love. He was crestfallen and heartbroken.

"She was very happy and at extreme peace. She is with her parents, brother, and her Lord. You, my friend, have a long life to live, and much to do. You shall be a leader in the new movement sparked by The Awakening. She will be with you from afar. It has been awhile since I was in Atlantis, but I believe she will be able to guide you from her realm. Like a guiding or guardian angel! And there is someone downstairs who has always adored you! Much longer than your one passionate day with Sandy."

Winston smiled. Jackhammer knew. He had always known. From the first day Savannah had told him about her young protégé. But then she was seriously ill. And gone. But now she was back.

Jackhammer walked into Room 1008 to pay his last respects to the woman of his end of the world romance. Apart

from the romance, he had always been respectful of and re-
liant on her sternness on the job, keeping him a tiny bit in
check on his uproarious commentary, but amused by her
sly sense of humor, and quick grin in any contentious moment. He would truly miss her.

As he walked to her former and now current bed, he was
perplexed. There did not appear to be a body under the
sheets. He pulled back the sheet, expecting to see her departed face. He gasped. He only saw a pillow. He wondered
if the white light had brought her back to life. Or if she returned from the Portal with its healing powers to complete
this life on a mission for The Awakening. He had hope.

Winston put his arm around Jackhammer's shoulder.

"It is a miracle. It happened after all the kids left the
room. She went through the Portal, body and all. This is
exciting both for religion and for science. I will let Savannah know. She will be thrilled about the living proof of her
hypotheses. Sandy is well, I am sure! Now, announce to the
crowd that the next set of helicopters and bright white
lights are not aliens!"

With that Winston headed down to the ninth floor.

Jackhammer followed his assignment.

15.

ECCA WATCHED THE KIDS ON THE NINTH floor bask in the white light. They all stood still for a long moment. Soon they were surrounded by ten screaming, shouting, joyously happy kids who had slid down the slide to the ninth floor. They pumped fists and hugged and laughed. The ninth-floor kids were still very ill. Most were delirious in the moment. One little girl became anxious that she would fall just short in time. Three times she had gone into remission. Three times her insidious lung disease returned. She passed out as her fear overwhelmed her.

Winston stopped and looked out the window on the midway point on the staircase to the ninth floor, where the steps took a 180 degree turn. He looked through the white painted wood framed panes. He could see the crowds pressing forward from Kenmore Square. And the crowds beyond were pressing, too. He saw that west of the hospital more crowds were hustling towards the hospital. He saw a squadron of Boston police cars. They were paralyzed in foot traffic. Winton knew the President was coming. He realized the Presidential helicopter had nowhere to land, save the Charles River. That would buy him some time to finish his mission.

Winston grabbed Becca's hand, and then Savannah. He shouted out Alleluia! The kids responded. Soon all the ninth-floor kids surrounded the three of them, touching and grabbing them wherever they could. John the Baptist watched in glee. Winston whispered his sayings into one little girl's ear. She in turn passed the message around. Winston then let out an uncharacteristic roar. Again, white light filled the room. The ninth-floor kids roared back and were soon joined in a chorus of song by the tenth-floor kids. Jackhammer smiled at Becca. She smiled and flipped her hair back. Winston smiled in amusement. Winston saw one little girl passed out in the corner. She was barely breathing. Again, he saw a thin thread of life. He hustled to her side and placed his hand on her chest. Soon, she inhaled large breaths of air. Her insidious lung disease was gone. She laughed out loud. All the kids turned and stared. This was the girl that could only wheeze. They joined her in laughter.

Winston followed all the kids down the slide to the eighth floor. Anna had used the SAKPORT to tell the kids on floors three through seven to meet on floor eight. The floor was packed. Fifty sick kids, and thirty from the third, ninth and tenth floors that were recently healed. Fourteen nurses from floors three to nine were there, as well as two new young nurses. The rest of the nurses initially could not recognize the two youthful nurses from the tenth floor. Quickly word spread. Jackhammer was there.

Winston healed all the nurses. More importantly, they all regained thirty years of youth. They raised their arms above their heads and hummed. Soon, all eighty kids, ten from each floor, did the same. Winston's powers were now enormous. He knew the Portal was near and feeding his power. Maybe the Atlantean crystals were in Boston as well as London. He did not recall or think about a Portal when he was in London. Maybe there was one there all along. He liked multiple explanations. The Atlantean crystals, the Portal, the Holy Spirit, the grace of the Lord. His body was becoming translucent. His hair was white with a silvery glow and shoulder length now. His beard had grown. It was white, too.

Winston raised his arms above his head, too. He belted out his healing words. He touched one child, and soon energy bolted through their bodies, and white light burst into their eyes. He heard a thunderous roar outside. There was Jackhammer, with a live feed for the world to watch and hear. Winston did not care about his anonymity now. He sensed he was not long for Boston, the cradle of The Awakening. A thought slipped through his earthly mind. "AH, no more golf!"

All eighty kids were fully healed. All sixteen nurses were healed and rejuvenated. Winston found some other staff members and maintenance crew. Their wounds, injuries, and maladies evaporated. All the kids and nurses and staff now slid down the slide. They poured out onto the sidewalk in front of the hospital, and then onto Commonwealth Avenue. Thousands of smartphones recorded the historic, miraculous occasion. Unbelievably, the burgeoning, crushing crowd had left room for the kids.

The raised their arms above their heads, as if they were in a concert, waving them to and fro. The massive crowd responded in kind.

Pockets of the crowd competed to start singing one song in unison. The star-spangled banner, and God Bless America gained some traction. Amazing Grace, and then Joy to the World took over for a while, then there was just a cacophony of dozens of songs. People were packed together, all the way from the hospital back to the Boston Common and the Public Gardens, on both Beacon Street and Commonwealth Avenue. Packed the other direction down Commonwealth Avenue. Packed on Brookline Avenue. Packed at the financial district and the seaport district.

Winston heard the big helicopter land on the Charles River. And then four more landed. He made his move.

Before the giant crowd he stood. He raised his arms. The crowd of hundreds of thousands stood quiet. There were now no voices, or chants, or even humming. Total silence. A soft breeze swirled in around the quiet former revelers. Jackhammer's smartphone was steadfast, just a few feet away. Savannah had her arm around the healer's left side, Becca had her arm around his right side. John the Baptist stood behind him, bracing him.

The Presidential helicopter and the other four others sat on the Charles River. The crowd remained silent, but it opened like the red sea. The President and the religious leaders soon stood within twenty feet of the healer. He walked over and whispered into each of their ears, other than the President. They each bowed and knelt. Soon the entire crowd followed suit and bowed and knelt.

Winston whispered one more time to the President. He beamed. Winston touched his chest. The President was healed. But more importantly, he knew and accepted his mission.

Winston then raised his arms to the sky. The same white light that fed from the sky a night ago returned in the grandest of luminescence. All in the crowd locked arms. All hundreds of thousands were connected.

"INFUSED BY THE HOLY SPIRIT, POWERED BY THE CRYSTALS OF ATLANTIS AND THE HIGHER SPIRITU- AL REALMS AND UNIVERSAL FORCE, AND FILLED WITH THE GRACE OF THE LORD, AS FORMER KING OF ATLANTIS, I SAY THAT YOU SHALL BE HEALED. SO IT SHALL BE SAID, SO IT SHALL BE DONE. GO AND

SERVE THE COMMON GOOD. THE AWAKENING HAS BEGUN. HERE IN BOSTON!"

With that, energy bolted through the hearts and minds of all hundreds of thousands in the crowd. White light burst into their eyes. All were healed. It was the most massive miracle in earth history. They all wept in joy. Billions around the world watched in joy. Boston, the birthplace of the world's greatest nation, was now the birthplace of The Awakening.

Winston slipped away quickly and returned to the tenth floor to Room 1108. There he saw the Portal. And he saw the face of the Lord.

16.

BECCA SAT across the table from Jackhammer, on Saturday morning. The massive crowds had dispersed. The President had taken all ten kids from the tenth floor back with him to the White House. Anna's Grandmother made the trip as well. She had been healed from afar by the healer, with the strong bond of Anna guiding him. St. Savannah was at her university furiously writing her masterpiece on the multiverse. A fellow from Palo Alto was arriving shortly to meet her. Santa and the elf were on national talk shows, as were all of the nurses from St. Aloysius Hospital. Debate and discourse filled all forms of the media on a global basis. The Pope was on a private jet from the Vatican to Boston. The world religious leaders stayed for a world summit in Boston, the Cardinal attending for the Pope until he arrived. John the Baptist was invited to the summit. He had a new girlfriend, too, the tenth-floor nurse. St. Aloysius Hospital was closed and declared a national monument. Thousands were attempting to heal their families and friends, with some success, with residual energy emanating from their bodies. The receptionist at the hospital was on her way to Hollywood in a private jet to star in a new motion picture.

"Where do you think the healer is? He disappeared after the Greatest Miracle! And his wife, London daughter, and Boston daughter are now in London with the Queen, without him," Becca mused.

"I think I feel his spirit. And that of Sandy. Maybe the world where they reside is right here near us. Who knows now. But I believe he went back through the Portal, pulled safely back by the Holy Spirit. He is in Atlantis! Or Heaven!"

"Oh, let the debates begin. Or an alien world! Or Parallel Universe! Alleluia!"

"Yes, The Awakening has begun! It began in Boston. Where our nation was born!"

Postscript

The author's pen name is King Atlas V. King Atlas V was once an Olympic hero in Atlantis. He later became King of Atlantis in its final months to save the continent from destruction. He did not succeed. Atlantis was a highly developed and technologically sophisticated society. In the 2020s and beyond mankind will match that success in technology. Hopefully, mankind will not make the same mistakes as the people of Atlantis did.

ABOUT THE AUTHOR

The author now lives in Florida with his wife of over thirty years. He has keen interests in the future, legends and myths, the dream world, alternate realities, healers and sports. He writes of the dreams of the fantastic and the mythical, so that others can enjoy those dreams. Check out other books written by the author at:
https://www.amazon.com/author/kingatlasv.